Silencing Outspoken Ambrosine

Silencing Outspoken Ambrosine

J. C. Walton

RESOURCE *Publications* · Eugene, Oregon

SILENCING OUTSPOKEN AMBROSINE

Resource Publications
An Imprint of Wipf and Stock Publishers
199 W. 8th Ave., Suite 3
Eugene, OR 97401

www.wipfandstock.com

PAPERBACK ISBN: 978-1-6667-6790-2
HARDCOVER ISBN: 978-1-6667-6791-9
EBOOK ISBN: 978-1-6667-6792-6

03/29/23

Contents

1. Fascinating Fossils | 1

2. A Mind-Blowing Moment | 6

3. A Fishy Story and a Droll Encounter | 9

4. The Chains Walk Challenge | 18

5. Tensions at the Warden's Traditional Tea | 23

6. Family Failings | 29

7. Tavern Tête-à-Tête | 35

8. Betrayed | 40

9. Tangling with Trees | 45

10. Benedict Hall Autumn Ball | 50

11. A Puerile Prank | 55

12. Toughing it Out | 59

13. Olympia as Scientist and Socialite | 64

14. Transforming Times | 71

15. Christmas Excursion | 76

16. Row Over Research | 81

17. Lunch with the Amhursts | 85

18. The Fossil Field Trip | 95

19. Fair and Foul in Conflict | 105

20. The Fossil Exhibition | 109

21. Machinations at MoliMart | 113

22. Drugs and Dismissal | 118

23. The Disappearance of Ambi | 124

24. Peril at Pleasant Park | 128

25. Aftermath | 135

26. Opportunities and Omens | 141

27. Fake Research and Faith Seminar | 147

28. Mrs. Maggs Amazes | 150

29. Ends and Beginnings | 158

Chapter 1. **Fascinating Fossils**

TALL, BROAD-SHOULDERED RUSSELL MARSHALL had fossils on his mind as he walked purposefully down the main street of Columburgh. Intriguing and enigmatic witnesses to life in the far past, they had always fascinated him. He'd gathered a small collection and was always looking out for more. To feed his hobby, he'd decided to enroll in an introductory course on paleontology. *Evolution is such a wonderfully imaginative and compelling way of understanding nature,* he thought to himself, as he made his way to the main biology lecture theater of Excelsis University. Everything fitted together so beautifully: from the Big Bang to stars and planets thence to bacteria and finally to primates. *It's a privilege to be at the pinnacle of Nature's chaotic creativity,* he mused. Russell was working toward a doctorate in biochemistry at Excelsis University.

Situated in the small town of Columburgh near the northeast coast of Britain, the illustrious institution had been founded in the sixteenth century and still maintained many unique traditions. It was recognized as top of the academic tree by all knowledgeable people. Russell had chosen to work for his Ph.D. there because of its outstanding reputation.

Because of her celebrity status, he'd decided to take the course on fossils offered by Prof. Olympia Sheldrake-Smith. That Wednesday he found a seat near the back of the large sloping theater and watched as it filled to capacity with animated students. Promptly on time, Prof. Olympia made her entrance, holding her laptop and, intriguingly, she had a tattered black book under one arm. She wore a black top with short, ruched sleeves over a white shirt showing her shapely cleavage. A short black skirt and strappy sandals completed the outfit. Her dark shoulder length hair showed hardly any grey and framed a strong face with an expression of confidence and authority. A good-looking woman, she radiated a strong sense of presence. Russell immediately understood her popularity with the media.

The students fell silent as she connected up her computer, greeted the class, and confidently introduced her topic. She screened pictures of pioneer paleontologists Georges Cuvier and Carl Linnaeus, who had invented the systems for naming and classifying biological species. Then, picking up her tattered old book, she strode forward with a broad smile, telling the students it was a Bible. Raising it above her head, she threw it dramatically to the floor. Then, spurning the tumbled pages with her shoe, she declared, "Before this course is over, you will all know this is nothing but a book of fables and fiction, designed to enslave the ignorant and gullible." Scattered laughter and a few hand claps spread among the students as she walked back to her computer.

Murmurs of surprise broke out as a girl sitting near the front raised her hand to ask a question. When indicated to go ahead, she said, "Are you saying we should approach paleontology in an emotionally charged way, with a blind commitment to evolution and loathing for religion?" Coming from an undergraduate, it had the flavor of a challenge. A ripple of expectant unease swept through the lecture hall. Prof. Olympia looked far from pleased to have her theatrical sound bite undermined.

"Paleontology is the prime discipline that completely confirms Darwin's theory of evolution through the successions of fossils," she replied loudly. Looking coldly at the girl, she continued, "As this course proceeds you will realize that nobody in their right mind questions the validity of Neo-Darwinism."

After the beautifully presented lecture, Russell faced a cold autumnal wind as he made his way along the cobbled main street of Columburgh to the biochemistry laboratories. The east end of Columburgh was situated on a high cliff overlooking a rocky shoreline. Atop the cliff huddled the ruins of a medieval castle. The town itself sprawled roughly west down narrow streets. A cluster of university buildings, both medieval and modern, flanked the castle. Others occupied choice locations round the town with the more modern departments situated further out west. The biochemistry laboratories, where Russell was working, stood towards the west end of the main street.

He was doing research on the folding of proteins, particularly those associated with the ends of chromosomes. It was demanding work, partly because of the complexity of the structures and instrumentation, but also because the proteins degraded so quickly and easily. The research group leader, Sir George Faircross, was a world expert on proteins. Having little patience and expecting experiments to work the first time, he would come down hard on anyone in his lab who didn't maintain a good flow of results.

Entering the lab, Russell spotted postdoctoral researcher Zemki Illovian in the far corner. Zemki was a rather strange character. Some days he was very friendly and helpful to the other researchers, other times he could be offhand and distant. Secretive about his own research, he preferred to work at night and carefully locked away all his notebooks and his protein separation gel traces. His projects were phenomenally successful. Time after time he came up with beautifully consistent protein data that either confirmed or extended Sir George's pet theories. A favorite with Faircross, he was an active member of the local sceptics' society.

Zemki was just carrying a piece of apparatus to another room and didn't notice Russell entering. As Russell walked past the fume hood where Illovian had been working, he noticed the open page of his lab notebook and immediately recognized the basic structure of the "roofie" drug Rohypnol, but with a subtle difference. Its structure had an added group that Russell knew could aid bio absorption and make it more potent. *Why would Zemki be interested in a date rape drug like that?* Russell wondered, as he headed to his own research space. Surely it had nothing to do with Zemki's protein research? Was he thinking of making the drug himself and selling it? That was ridiculous, Russell told himself. Pushing the thought aside, he spent the afternoon using some advanced software he had developed himself, first probing 3D protein structures, then starting the experiment he had just designed.

That evening, as he walked back to Benedict Hall, the student residence where he was a sub-warden, he drank in the gorgeous yellows and russets of the autumn foliage and stopped to smell the red dog roses in the hedge adjacent to the residence gateway. Although he nearly fell afoul of an impatient bee gathering nectar, he considered the risk worthwhile for the incomparable scent. *How could the biochemistry underlying the beautiful, variegated colors, scents, and bee pollination of roses have evolved together spontaneously?* he mused. He made a mental note to look up proposed evolutionary pathways at the next opportunity.

Benedict Hall was adjacent to the central quadrangle of Excelsis University and close to Columburgh town center. It had been built of stone in the charming, serene style of the nineteen thirties. Mounting the stone steps, he walked through the ornamental gatehouse, unlocked the massive oak door with his key card, and pushed it open. He looked approvingly round the wood-paneled and stone flagged vestibule, picked up his mail, and went upstairs to his study-bedroom. It was part of his job to provide guidance and support to the younger students, help make their stay safe, and foster a community spirit. Benedict was a long-established residence that still kept up its time-honored traditions, including the gowned procession to Chapel on Sundays and weekly Warden's Tea occasions. Such events encouraged social intercourse and helped to make a tight knit community. Later, Russell came down to the dining hall and, as usual, looked admiringly at its beautiful wood paneling and the serried stained-glass windows depicting former college benefactors.

An unfussy eater, he collected a simple meal of crispy haddock and chips with garden peas. Emerging into the main hall, he eyed the tables and saw Roger Mason, known as 'Slab,' from his muscular build and pugnacious attitude, sitting with his current girl, Veronica Mortlake, and a group of friends. Slab had limitless self-confidence derived from his wealthy banking family and from the fearsome reputation he enjoyed as a star member of the university judo team. He was wearing a black T-shirt emblazoned with the slogan "Always Right," accompanied with the usual blue jeans and tennis shoes. Veronica had on a blue and white striped crop top that showed a good deal of midriff. Part of a tattoo, placed close to her heart, was visible. It depicted Darwin's original spiky Tree of Life. She had on shredded jeans and dangly earrings matching a thin golden necklace carrying the message, "Go Ape."

As Russell sat beside them, he could hear them discussing Prof. Olympia's lecture. "She's a super cool Prof.," Veronica was saying, "and her PowerPoint graphics of fossil trilobites were amazing."

"Yeah," Slab replied, "but that stupid girl interrupting with those silly questions of hers needs taking care of. Does anyone know who she is?"

Veronica's friend Anna Bellamy chipped in. "She's staying in this Hall along the corridor from me, but I haven't got acquainted with her yet."

Before the conversation could go any further, Russell interjected, as he faced Veronica, "It's good to have evolution theory presented so persuasively by Prof. Olympia. But what did you think of her Bible bashing stunt? Was that a wise gesture in front of such a varied group?"

"I loved it!" Veronica exclaimed. "Those dusty old religious books are nothing but fables. It's high time society shook off the chains of religious bigotry. I'm all for celebrity figures like Olympia telling things the way they really are."

Using as many sibilants as he could manage, Slab's hanger-on Oliver Oaten lisped, "Ess, we says she speak smart." He'd watched the *Lord of the Rings* film trilogy multiple times, was fascinated by Gollum, and usually tried to model his speech on the character. Out of his hearing, he was known as Nollum.

"Do you think she's one of those angry new atheists?" Russell asked.

"Yeah, probably," Slab replied self-assuredly. "Dawkins and Hitchens write brilliant stuff. She probably moves in their circles when she isn't dazzling us guys here at Excelsis."

Veronica fluttered her eyes as she asked Russell, "Are you going to stick with Prof. Olympia's course?"

"Definitely. I've always found fossils fascinating! Each one has a story to tell about its owner's way of life and how it met its end. Paleontology opens a window on the full panoply of life back into the distant past and helps us understand our own roots. Furthermore," he added, "most of us will get a chance to go on her field trip later in the year to get firsthand experience of fossil hunting and how to collect and preserve them. That should be a unique experience, particularly as Prof. Olympia will be coming along as well."

"Yeah," Slab chuckled confidently, "I can't wait for the opportunity to get up close to a hottie like her."

Chapter 2. **A Mind-Blowing Moment**

THAT WEEK, RUSSELL WORKED steadily at his protein folding research project. Using his own designer software, he probed the intimate structures of the chromosomes of more and more different species. He focused on the "telomere" protein segments at the ends of each species' chromosomes. One day he had a Eureka moment. At least, he hoped it was one. He noticed that the molecular structure of a repeating unit in almost all the telomere proteins bore a striking resemblance to that of an unrelated enzyme known as *longiferase*. The structures looked complementary, so he had an idea that *longiferase* might "dock" and merge with a similar protein called *telomerase,* known to be an especially efficient broad-spectrum catalyst for protein repair. *Longiferase* was much more accessible than *telomerase* which could only be obtained from stem cells. If docking happened, *longiferase* could well help extend the ends of telomeres. In that way old telomeres might re-grow, enabling the restoration of chromosome activity in the elderly.

Excitedly, Russell opened up the *FlexDoc* docking software on his computer and started loading the structural data for *telomerase* and *longiferase* enzymes. He set the input parameters and watched as the calculation proceeded. The screen showed slices of the resulting merged structure as the two enzymes approached each other from various angles. Visually it seemed clear to Russell that the fit was good. Furthermore, the software outputted very satisfactory correlation criteria. Russell knew that enzyme structures were highly flexible and susceptible to the amount of water and any ions present. Different types of docking software handled such flexing and folding in more or less sophisticated ways. As a cross-check, during the next few days he tried matching the two structures with other different types of docking programs. The majority of cases produced high matching statistics. Russell's interest and enthusiasm grew as the probability of the match increased.

Somehow sensing his excitement, Zemki came over to Russell's area one afternoon and tried to see what he was doing. "How are your protein folding experiments proceeding?" he asked. Russell was a bit dubious about Illovian, because of his secretiveness and extraordinary success. Seeing the modified Rohypnol structure in Zemki's notebook had deepened his unease. However, he didn't want to antagonize someone who was Sir George's favorite and right-hand man. Standing in front of his screen, he explained, "I'm docking the *telomerase* structure with various molecules and testing the reliability of different types of docking software. It's a slow process, because of the flexibility problem, but I'm finding that, though it's free to use, the *FlexDoc* app is just about as good as the more sophisticated commercial apps available to us. Do you think it might be worth our while to produce a streamlined second-generation version, say *FlexPlus*, and market it?" Since Zemki was an experimental biochemist with no interest in computer programming, the conversation soon languished, and he wandered back to his own research area. From then onward, Russell always took his laptop and notes back to Benedict Hall with him.

That evening, while walking back to Benedict Hall, he happened to observe Slab and Veronica strolling ahead of him. As he was idly watching, he noticed Slab "accidently" knock over the paper cup containing the collected coins of a beggar woman sitting beside a shop entrance. The couple continued on, laughing as the few coins rolled aimlessly around. Instinctively, Russell darted forward, retrieved the cup, and started to gather the coins. Returning the cup to the crying woman, he added a pound coin from his own pocket.

Glancing over their shoulders, Slab and Veronica saw what he was doing. Slab turned back, saying loudly, "These people are all bogus bums and professional beggars from Eastern Europe. They should all rabbit off home or get jobs."

"Leave her alone," Russell retorted. "This poor woman may well be a professional beggar, but she's still a human being. She deserves to be treated with dignity, not rudeness." Slab moved off, scowling and muttering something about parasites plaguing society. Reaching into his pocket, Russell added another pound from his own meagre funds, smiled at the now calm woman, and walked on.

Later that evening he checked *Wikipedia* and then various textbooks for explanations of how flowers and bees had evolved. He read that the widespread appearance of flowering plants about 100 million years ago just fortunately coincided with the appearance of bee pollinators. The two groups both need pollen, the sources stated, so they co-evolved for mutual success. He had hoped to find an explanation of why bees picked up mutations to their DNA that created special flight muscles and special hairs on their bodies, just at the same time as plants developed color, odor, shape, size, and nectar specially designed to attract bees. Finally, he had to conclude that the various accounts of flower and bee origins were pretty much wishful thinking. They all relied on masses of serendipity.

Chapter 3. **A Fishy Story and a Droll Encounter**

Амви Амhurst was standing pensively in her room in Benedict Hall, preparing for Olympia Sheldrake-Smith's Wednesday paleontology lecture. Outside, gray clouds scudded threateningly across the sky. Cold showers alternated with short intervals of sunshine. The unsettled weather matched her mood. She was wondering if she had made a mistake in opting to study geoscience and paleontology at Excelsis. So far, apart from Sarah McBride, who had been at school with her and had chosen the same university, she had made few friends. Ostensible Christians were few on campus, or at least were keeping a low profile. The student Christian Union seemed full of shallow happy-clappy types. She had joined the Benedict Hall Christian Association, but so far, they seemed overly fixated on politically correct themes such as diversity, animal rights, and climate change. The students in her geoscience course seemed mostly to be agnostics or atheists with apparently closed minds on questions of origins or faith.

For a few moments she considered the males she had met so far. Slab Mason was tall, strong, and handsome but he was as sociable as a bull in a China shop, and so high on testosterone that he gave her the creeps. His friend Oliver, with his morbid fixation on Gollum, made her even more uneasy. Believing that he needed urgent counselling, she determined to stay clear of both of them as much as she could. For a moment she wondered if her father, Pastor John Amhurst, had been right in suggesting that she stay at home, marry that nice guy Daniel Smith, and settle down to a life of motherhood and children. Daniel was good-looking, dependable, and had a stable job in an accountant's office. Although she knew he would be willing, somehow she felt there was no chemistry between them, let alone any biochemistry.

Thinking back to earlier in the week, she remembered being on the other side of the street and seeing Slab upset the beggar woman's coins. She had started to cross the road to offer help, but a tall attractive male student had moved in and restored the situation. He was obviously not intimidated by Slab's reputation as a Judo expert. Though she didn't catch what he had said, it had given Slab pause and even made him back off. The kindly gesture toward the ragged beggar woman had struck a chord with her, and she felt that she would like to get to know the young man. His appearance seemed vaguely familiar: could he be someone she had caught a glimpse of at Olympia's paleontology lecture?

It was time to start for the lecture hall. Checking her high half-pony hairstyle in her mirror, she pulled her plentiful glossy tresses forward to frame her face. She knew she was fortunate to have such abundant hair and didn't mind that it always seemed to go a bit wild. In the corridor, she greeted Mrs. Maggs, one of the Hall's cleaning ladies, and asked how she was doing. "I'm fine now, love," she said, "and thanks for the lovely grapes. Me and me nephew really enjoyed them." Elsie Maggs doted on her nephew, Arthur, and was constantly urging him to get a "proper" job. Ambi hurried on, seating herself one row from the front in the biology lecture theater.

Prof. Olympia arrived in good time as usual, wearing an outfit that seemed a bit inappropriate for an academic. Russell, seated near the back, wondered why she always felt the need to show so much bare flesh. She was a world-renowned expert on paleontology. So why did she always appear with body parts peeping from her outfits? The habit had earned her the nickname "Peepy" among some of the male students. Did it imply basic insecurity in her character? Was it a cry for attention and approval? But that seemed so unlikely! An attractive woman and a popular personality on the internet, she even appeared from time to time on mainline TV shows. She was at the top of her discipline and a star academic of Excelsis University. Was it then to emphasize that though she dwelt in the higher reaches of academia she was still a real woman? Or did she consider herself, as she often characterized her vertebrate specimens, simply a capsule of DNA struggling to survive and propagate? Was it her way of showing her DNA was available for coupling and spreading? Rumors circulated about her sexual behavior, but Russell discounted them as phony bragging.

He shelved such thoughts to concentrate on her account of the emergence of the first vertebrates on land. She was telling a dramatic story of how, in the late Devonian Period, the fins of a fish called *Tiktaalik* had evolved into more limb-like features. Some bolder ones had crawled onto land to catch insects, thus enabling natural selection to mold them from fish into the first amphibians. Her voice rose a pitch, as she described how their brave venture onto land proved to be a great leap of evolution, ultimately leading to the vast panoply of land-dwelling vertebrate creatures. On a note of triumph, she told of how Chicago and Harvard paleontologists Shubin, Daeschler, and Jenkins had used evolutionary theory to predict that such transitional fossils should be present in late Devonian strata. As her showpiece, she screened colorful graphics of the *Tiktaalik fossils* the paleontologists had triumphantly discovered on Ellesmere Island in Nunavut, Arctic Canada. The account and the artistic reconstructions of what the live fish might have looked like delighted Russell.

Olympia's elegant narrative flow was interrupted at this point. The same girl as before, sitting near the front, raised a hand to ask a question. Somewhat reluctantly Olympia assented, and the girl said, "Fish reproduction is a slippery process in which the male wraps his body around the female in a so-called 'nuptial embrace' that requires the support of water to achieve and maintain. How could the *Tiktaaliks* have reproduced on land? Furthermore, isn't it a fact that fossil footprints of undoubted quadrupeds have been discovered in much older strata: thus challenging *Tiktaaliks* as intermediates?" Her tone carried a note of skepticism.

For a moment Olympia looked taken aback, but she recovered quickly and replied, "Evolution and natural selection are incredibly powerful processes, and sometimes they work rapidly. It's perfectly reasonable to assume that fin, lung, and reproductive modifications were all assimilated into the *Tiktaalik* gene pool in a comparatively short time." Leaving no time for any response, she continued through to the end of her lecture.

The students streamed out of the theater, many heading for the student common room for a morning coffee. When Russell headed there too, he saw the irritating girl surrounded by a group of excited students. Russell had taken a dislike to the girl with her ignorant and niggling questions. He saw she was slim and of medium height with a mass of unruly hair. As he approached the group, he heard Slab telling her to leave Olympia alone and stop interrupting her lectures with senseless questions.

"I came to Excelsis expecting a place where freedom of speech would be prized and where questions would be encouraged," she calmly replied. "I'm not so sold on orthodox evolutionary dogma. I've many honest questions about origins."

Veronica's friend Anna interrupted, saying, "Evolutionary theory is as well established as the earth revolving around the sun! Questioning it just wastes time. Surely, you're not one of those bigoted fundamentalist Christians, are you?"

"If evolution has the facts, what is there to fear?" she replied. "I'm disappointed to find discussion always being squashed. Instead of answers, I'm fobbed off by name calling, such as 'bigot' or 'ignorant.' What's more, Prof. Olympia ignores questions, and when she occasionally answers, it is simply with unsupported assertions. That's exactly what happened this morning with her claims about the power and speed of *Tiktaalik* evolution."

The calm assurance of the girl gave her listeners pause. They were not happy to hear criticism of such a celebrity as Olympia, but they sensed that what the girl was saying did have some validity. "I doubt if Olympia's lectures are the place for such questions," Russell interjected. "You should raise those points during tutorials or check them out in textbooks."

"I get exactly the same impatient treatment in tutorials," the girl, still unfazed, replied. "What's more, Olympia is only repeating what's already in the textbooks. They usually make confident but unsubstantiated assertions when it comes to critical issues." By this time, the group had begun breaking up to go to other classes.

By now Ambi had recognized the young man as the one who had helped the beggar woman. His comments disappointed her. Furthermore, he had looked at her in a cold, disapproving way and seemed to join all the others in their refusal to even listen to questions about evolutionary dogma. As she headed to her next geoscience lecture, she felt it would be impossible to make a friend of him.

For his part, though, Russell felt somewhat mollified by the reasonable answers the girl had given. She had frank honest eyes in an innocent face that, he thought, gave her a rare, unworldly look of purity. It further impressed him how unafraid she seemed when confronted by a hostile group of her peers. However, he put such thoughts out of his mind as he hurried along the leaf-strewn streets to his biochemistry lab.

Excited about his recent discovery, Russell felt sure it could be a highly significant finding in relation to human longevity. Several academic and commercial research institutes had been expanding their programs in this area. Cells divide only 40 to 60 times, a sequence known as the Hayflick limit, before they stop. At each division, the telomeres on the ends of each of a cell's chromosomes shorten slightly. Then human cells enter the senescence phase, thus restricting human longevity. However, it had been discovered that, after introducing the *telomerase* enzyme into the diets of microorganisms, worms, and flies, their cells continued to divide well beyond the Hayflick limit. Researchers had observed lifetimes of up to five times as long as normal for the various species.

The *telomerase* enzyme reduced the loss of telomere proteins and so enabled cell reproduction to continue. The idea that it might enable human cell division to exceed the Hayflick limit greatly excited him. Claims that human lifespan could thereby be extended indefinitely had begun to appear. Russell knew that hundreds of millions of dollars was being ploughed into bio-gerontology labs for research along such lines. A problem was the scarcity of the *telomerase* material which could only be obtained from stem cells harvested from embryos. His *longiferase* discovery might circumvent the problem. Up till now his doctoral research had been on a humdrum project originally designed by Sir George Faircross. But Russell thought *longiferase* could supercharge his research into internationally attention-grabbing status.

As he mulled over the idea during the next few days, and examined various ramifications of it, he concluded it would need major resources to thoroughly investigate. He would require access to protein synthesis equipment, refrigerated centrifuges, ultrasonic cell disintegrators, and gel electrophoresis, together with expensive biochemicals. Furthermore, the synthesized materials would have to be tested, first using microorganism-based assays, but eventually with lab animals. Some, but by no means all of the resources, were available in Sir George's lab. However, he would have to approach Faircross and get his approval and backing. He sent him an email asking for an appointment.

During the next few days, he kept research on his protein folding work ticking over but spent hours thinking about his *longiferase* project. He examined its 3D structure in minute detail, planning how it might be synthesized. Then he considered possibilities for variants with modified, even better properties. After checking commercial sources of the needed starting materials, he looked over potentially useful bioassays.

Health and fitness were important aspects of Russell's life. Careful about his consumption of alcohol, he regularly went to the gym for workouts. Because he recognized that speed of reaction was critical in most sports, he always included juggling routines with balls and BlazePod Drills specially designed to improve his reaction times.

Throughout his life Russell had had a lifelong habit of investigating those things he came across that interested or intrigued him. That afternoon he looked up *Tiktaaliks* on the internet and found that indeed their position as transitional fossils was highly controversial. Furthermore, he read that several trackways, credited to four-limbed animals, had really been uncovered in older strata at a place called Zachelmie in Poland. The discoverers insisted that they proved that four-footed animals had appeared long before *Tiktaalik*. The girl's question had been genuine and intelligent. He concluded that Prof. Olympia had been exaggerating. She had put a spin on the *Tiktaalik* data that it didn't really deserve. Then he began to wonder if she was doing the same thing with other material in her lectures.

Russell's appointment with Sir George Faircross was early the next day. Collecting his laptop and papers, he made his way to Sir George's office on the top floor of the biochemistry building. In peaceful contrast to the busy and spartan laboratory conditions below, the office was luxuriously carpeted and lined on two sides with carved wooden bookcases filled with leather-bound volumes, as well as selected periodicals. The windows on two sides gave magnificent views of countryside, golf courses, and the distant seashore. Several gold-framed pictures that appeared to be original modern abstract style oil paintings hung on the walls. One, with the title "Staffa," showed a jumble of multicolored hexagonal shapes. Another, with the title "Evolution," displayed a welter of struggling bodies, and Russell thought it owed its inspiration to Gustav Vigeland's monolithic sculpture of tangled figures in Oslo. The windows let sunlight splash across Sir George's large executive desk with its gold-decorated ornaments.

Faircross, a tall man tending to portliness, was in his early fifties with slightly graying hair and a neatly trimmed short, boxed beard. He had dark piercing eyes that seemed to look deeply into everything. As always, he was dressed in a smart business suit. Greeting Russell in a friendly way, he asked how his project was proceeding. Diplomatically, Russell started with a description of what he had achieved on the protein folding experiments that Sir George had originally designed. Then he moved on to his visualization software and of the match between the *telomerase* and *longiferase* structures it had enabled him to discover. To demonstrate what he had found, he showed a set of graphics of the structures on his laptop that illustrated how well they corresponded. He was sure Sir George would recognize the implications for longevity research but proceeded anyway to hit the highlights.

The older man listened attentively and interjected comments and questions, but gave no sign of either approval or rejection. When Russell had finished, Sir George said, "You must give me time to think this over carefully. There are multiple angles and implications, and any such project would require large allocations of resources." Considering such an observation perfectly reasonable, Russell was satisfied to leave it with Faircross for the time being. As he was leaving, Sir George said, "I'll see you at the Sceptics Meeting this evening then?" He meant the Society of Pyrrhonian Sceptics that held monthly meetings in Columburgh. Members had a perverse sort of pride in the acronym SOPYS often applied to them. "This evening will start with a showing of a presentation by Christopher Hitchens expounding his book *God is Not Great*."

"I'll certainly be there," Russell said as he exited the office.

That evening he headed to the Sceptics meeting in the College Hall adjacent to the main University quadrangle. The society had begun back in the 1960s, following a visit by Bertrand Russell to Excelsis University. Russell Marshall's father, Karl, had been one of the founder members, and Russell's own name had sprung from the same event. The society was named after the first ancient Greek school of skepticism established by Pyrrho of Elis. Twenty or thirty people were present as Hitchens talked on screen in his usual energetic way. It was entertaining stuff. Judged by the comments in the discussion afterwards, the confirmed atheists in the audience highly approved of the presentation. However, it bothered Russell that Hitchens lumped all religions into the same despicable category, and that he ignored the real history of religious thought. His dismissal of all biblical history and smearing of all Christian activities struck him as less than honest. Hitchens wasn't a good example of the intellectual integrity and rational outlook his father had so often told him distinguished atheists from the hypocritically dishonest Christians.

A couple of days later a wild autumn storm blew in from the east. All night, clouds scudded across the sky, winds howled round Benedict Hall, and rain spattered the windows. It was still stormy when Russell got up and prepared for breakfast. His windows had been tightly shut all night, but he unlatched one to air the room. Opening his door, he saw

Mrs. Maggs right outside just preparing to knock. At that very moment, the door at the end of the corridor also opened and a group of students came through on their way to the dining hall. A strong gust of wind drove through his window, and augmented by the open door of the corridor, it swung Russell's door rapidly shut, propelling him forward and into Mrs. Maggs. The two of them toppled over.

Russell's quick reflexes enabled him to get a hand behind her head before they hit the floor, preventing, he hoped, any serious injury. The banging doors and student exclamations had roused others, and hearing the commotion, more students, including Ambi and Sarah, arrived from other parts of the Hall to see what was going on. They were astonished to find Russell, sprawled on top of a squealing Mrs. Maggs, apparently with an arm clasped round her.

Inevitably, it was Slab who shouted, "There are bedrooms for that stuff, why make an exhibition of yourselves in the corridor?"

Mrs. Maggs recovered quickly as Russell helped her to her feet. "None of your impudence and mind your own business," she shot at Slab.

With a mischievous look, Veronica said to Russell, "You'll have to do the decent thing now and marry her." Overtaken with the humor of the situation, Russell could hardly control his laughter. "I guess you're right. Has anybody got a ring?" he asked the onlookers, "but I doubt if Mrs. Maggs would have me?"

She looked consideringly at Russell. "It's a tempting offer, love, but it would be bigamy. We'd better not rush into anything we can't finish."

The onlookers began to drift down to breakfast animatedly discussing the incident. None of them had seen the whole thing, so mystery shrouded it. Wildly speculative accounts circulated during the next few weeks. Mrs. Maggs achieved minor celebrity status as a "femme fatale" among the more gullible students. Ambi was as puzzled as anyone. She hadn't regarded Russell as that type of womanizer at all. And Mrs. Maggs, though well preserved, was surely old enough to be his mother. The saying "there's nowt so queer as folk" took on a new meaning for her. Although she suspected there was more than had met her eyes in the incident, she decided the world was a much stranger place than she had heretofore realized.

After Russell helped Mrs. Maggs to her feet, he asked her twice if she felt OK. In spite of her assurances that she was fine, he insisted on holding her arm and guiding her to a seat in the vacant Warden's office. He fetched her a cup of tea and a buttered scone, then rang cleaning services, insisting they give her the morning off due to the accident. Somehow the incident built a bond between the two. Elsie Maggs felt touched by his concern and appreciative of the mystery status the incident had earned her. From that day forward the two always looked out for one another, something that would prove of fateful importance in the future.

Elsie Maggs dearly loved simple jokes and proverbs and usually greeted Russell in the mornings with one or the other. "Knock, knock," she might say, and when he answered, "Who's there?" she would come up with "Wooden shoe." To Russell's, "What do you mean wooden shoe?" she would retort, "Wooden shoe like to know!" Keeping his study-bedroom spotless, she made sure he never wanted for household items.

Chapter 4. The Chains Walk Challenge

DURING THE NEXT WEEK, Russell spent most days in the lab attending to his experiments, noting everything on his laptop, and planning his *longiferase* project. There seemed so much to do. Life was far too short to even touch the surface of his many projects or to explore all the many subjects he was interested in. He wondered idly why evolution couldn't have arranged, by natural selection, for much longer human lifespans. Longer-lived individuals, with their greater experience and memories filled with knowledge, would have greatly significant selective advantages over the rest. He knew ocean dwelling hydra could regenerate and so live practically forever. Other ocean species such as clams and sharks survived for many hundreds of years. Furthermore, the rings of certain trees showed they existed for thousands of years. As the epitome of evolutionary progress, he thought, *Homo sapiens* ought to have much longer life spans.

Russell was fond of personifying things. Calling to mind the three main drivers of evolution—Chance, Mutation, and Selection—he pictured them as the modern metamorphoses of the three Greek fate sisters, the Moirai goddesses, spinning out the destinies of life from their eyrie on Mount Olympus. In his imagination he saw three venerable evolutionary Moirai goddesses, seated at a celestial epicenter, establishing the destinies of every living kind. Fickle Chance was the modern counterpart of Clotho, drawing out threads of life from her inexhaustible chest of materials. Deadly Mutation corresponded with Atropos, the inexorable, allotting to each species a time of change and the manner of their extinction. Then, Russell thought, elite Selection was the reincarnation of Lachesis, the allotter, measuring to each species their specific thread of life, some short, some long. Why couldn't they have allotted to humankind the same unending lives as to the immortal gods? Or at least, in view of the billions of years of cosmic time, have endowed much longer life spans than a mere 70 years? But such images gave way to the wry thought that he'd better get moving and make the best use of whatever years remained to him.

Student traditions were an important feature of life at Excelsis. Russell was a member of an exclusive student society, the Chris Classicus Club, known colloquially as the CC Club. Christopher Classicus had been a student who, in the sixteenth century, had stood for increased student freedoms. He'd petitioned for students to be allowed sports on Sundays and a less restricted diet on Fridays. The Queen was patron of the University. Having outraged her piety, he had been put to death for his presumption. Various stories circulated about the beginnings of the club, but it had been in existence at least since the Victorian age. Its business was social and charitable and each year it organized the traditional student "chains walk."

Columburgh was situated close to the sea. Nearby a coastal pathway traversed the beaches and rock faces north and south of the town. Part of it involved sea cliffs, deep rocky inlets, and tall headlands. Because it was a challenging trail, back in Victorian times chains had been fastened to the steeper sections of the cliffs, around the sharper headlands, and across the ends of the most precipitous inlets. The chains had been renewed from time to time but, even with their help, a two-mile section of the walk was very difficult, especially when the tide was in and the waves rushed up the inlets and lashed the foot of the cliffs.

Intrepid first-year students would pay a fee for the privilege of competing in the autumn CC Club "chains walk challenge." Club members would pass among the crowds who came out to watch the start and finish of the walk, collecting contributions to donate to selected charities. Each participant would receive a number to wear and a printed map of the route. At the start of the walk club members would inspect their shoes and clothing to make sure they were appropriate and safe. Experienced climbers waited at the more dangerous places to help any participants in difficulty and escort back any who found the going too tough. The end of the walk was downhill from the cliffs, ending in a Columburgh car park. Students who successfully finished the walk received a certificate and a badge and were entitled to a snack meal provided in a tent erected for this purpose. The badges were highly prized, and the successful climbers proudly wore them. Only such badge holders were eligible to be considered for membership in the CC Club. Ambi was determined to enter the chains walk that coming Sunday. She talked it over with her friend Sarah who tried to dissuade her.

"It's absolutely exhausting," Sarah protested. "Nothing would persuade me to undertake it. Every year people come back with injuries and bruises. Sometimes bones get broken, and one terrible year a student fell into an inlet, drowned, and was swept out to sea."

But Ambi was undeterred. "I keep fit with regular workouts," she insisted. "Slab, Veronica, and that crowd are entering. I'm not going to let them crow over me! I'll have my mobile phone to call for assistance if I get in trouble. The CC Club post people to help you at the most difficult spots. Stop worrying and help me to decide what to wear." Lightweight, comfortable garments seemed best, so eventually Ambi selected a cotton T-shirt under a loose light weight fleece jacket in bright red, so that she would be easily visible. She chose her charcoal zip trousers with button-up pockets and her best pair of sturdy shoes with grippy soles.

Naturally cautious, Sarah was uneasy that Ambi could be biting off more than she could chew. She knew Daniel well and phoned him to let him know what Ambi was contemplating.

Shocked, he immediately contacted Ambi. "You know," he said ponderously, "I'm older and wiser than you, and I know what's best for you. That chains walk is not for delicate, carefully brought-up females like you. You must let yourself be guided by me and not go ahead with that silly scheme of yours. It may be OK for the tough guys, but it's not for you."

Inwardly, Ambi was furious at what he said. What gave him the right to claim any sort of authority over her? Although her father approved of him, she had never given him the least hint of special regard or encouragement. "Thanks for your timid advice, Daniel," she said, "but every year scores of students, female as well as male, successfully complete the walk. This year I intend to be one of them!" she added firmly.

"Now, hold your horses . . . ," he started to say.

But Ambi was in no mood to hear more, so she pressed her red "end call" button.

Sunday dawned a fine autumnal day, mostly cloudy but with occasional sunny periods. Thankfully, Ambi noted no rain was forecast. She donned her chosen gear, then meeting Sarah, they headed for the 10:00 a.m. start of the walk, close to the West Beach of the town. Already a fair-sized crowd had gathered to watch. Ambi collected her participant number and map from the CC Club tent. Pinning it to her top, she waited for her turn to start. To prevent crowding on the cliffs, the participants went one by one. Finally, her turn came. She gave Sarah her scarf and outer coat, noted the time on her watch, and set off up the cliff path. Light footed and nimble, she made good progress. The chains made the difficult sections much more doable. Rocky outcrops jutted into the gray-green sea, and breakers rolled up on the sand and into the rocky inlets. From time to time, she took pictures of the spectacular scenery with the smart phone she had brought with her. At first, she felt exhilarated by the beauty of the walk, the sound of the surf, and the cries of the sea birds.

After half an hour's climbing, she began to feel thirsty and regretted that she'd neglected to bring a water bottle with her. By now she was approaching the most difficult section known as "Wolf's Jaw." The inlet had steep cliffs on either side and was filled with jagged rocks around which water surged. Ambi had to inch along narrow ledges on either side while clinging to the chains. At one awkward fault in the rock face, her foot slipped off the ledge, and her heart skipped a beat as she hung grimly to the chain. Saying a quick prayer, she sought frantically for purchase with her foot, and mercifully re-found the ledge.

She could see a guy wearing CC Club identification on a nearby rocky vantage point. He had a collection of drink cartons to distribute to climbers. This was a welcome sight, so she approached to ask for one. The hoodie he wore prevented her from recognizing him until she was quite close, and then she involuntarily shrank back. It was the guy she had seen climbing off Mrs. Maggs the other day!

Noticing her hesitation, he asked, "Are you OK?"

Without thinking she exclaimed, "You're the guy that was trying to mount Mrs. Maggs!"

Laughingly, he replied, "You shouldn't believe all the rumors you hear circulating round Benedict Hall."

"I saw you getting off her!" she said accusingly.

Russell had decided the true explanation of the incident made him appear a clumsy oaf, so, he just said, "Appearances can be very deceptive. Elsie Maggs and I are simply good friends, nothing more. You had a close call back there in the Wolf's Jaw! Thank goodness the fanged beast couldn't claim another little Red Riding Hood!"

Ambi laughed as she fingered her red top, and even though he said no more about the Maggs' incident, somehow she felt reassured about him. Her instincts said he was no wolf. He had none of the manners or appearance of the predatory males she sometimes had to fight off.

"Would you like a carton of apple juice to help you recover?" he asked. Taking the carton, she thanked him politely and continued along the cliff path.

Resting for a few minutes on a grassy knoll, she took in the beauty of the changing cliff colors, the rock pools with their green seaweed, the blue harebells and purple sea thrift, the swaying bunches of marram grass, and the brilliant yellow gorse at the cliff tops. Gulls soared and glided on the air currents, sounding plaintive calls as the climbers disturbed them. Out to sea a small fishing boat ploughed through the waves, followed by a flock of swooping and diving birds. Some lines of poetry flitted through her mind: "Wayside flowers are the loveliest of all, dreaming their own unaided dreams, dancing to the rhythm of freedom's breeze, voicing their own distinctive call." She managed to get a selfie of herself clinging to one of the chains on a steep part of the cliff, then steadily continued to the end of the climb.

Tired but triumphant, she made her way down into the final car park where she could see Sarah and Daniel waiting to greet her. He looked thunderous. But first she handed her number in at the CC Club tent. After the official noted her climb time of one hour and twenty minutes, he presented her with the coveted badge on a ribbon to display round her neck. She had done it! When she joined in excitedly congratulating other successful students, Sarah rushed up and hugged her. "Congratulations! You aced the whole thing! You're a marvel!"

Daniel joined them, but all he reproachfully said was, "You're lucky to be unhurt. I hope you aren't overcome by strains and sprains in the next few days."

Ambi felt let down. "Aren't you going to congratulate me?" Seeing his ungracious expression, she said, "Well, the least you can do is to take a photo of me and Sarah with me holding my badge." As she and Sarah lined up in front of the CC tent, Ambi raised a triumphant fist and shouted, "Yay!" Daniel only looked even more disapproving.

Ambi re-entered the CC tent to collect her snack meal and shared it with Sarah and Daniel as they walked back to town. Her muscles ached that evening, but as she took a warm shower, she happily sang out loud, "God will take care of you, through every day, o'er all the way; He will take care of you, God will take care of you." She knew a good night's sleep would see her almost back to her normal self.

Chapter 5. **Tensions at the Warden's Traditional Tea**

VICTORIA SINCLAIR, THE WARDEN of Benedict Hall, had invited Russell to attend one of her traditional Warden's Teas the afternoon of the next day. Russell was slowly getting to know her and liking what he saw. She was a strong woman, determined to maintain the high reputation of Benedict Hall as the University's premier place for social and scholarly pursuits. Although ruthlessly terminating those who broke the rules, she steadfastly believed students were innocent until proven guilty. Any student in trouble knew they could rely on her for good advice, tangible help, and complete discretion. Because she was a stickler for good timing and for good grooming, Russell dressed carefully in neat, casual clothes. He arrived at the Warden's Day Room five minutes before the stipulated time. The décor reflected her lifelong interest in ancient Greek culture and lifestyle. The spotless white tablecloth on the eighteenth-century English Oak dining table was edged with a golden Greek meander pattern. On her walls she had framed photographic reproductions of two classically beautiful Greek amphorae. Adjacent, were pictures of the heads of important philosophers and of a Spartan woman handing a shield to her warrior husband.

All seven of the invited undergrads arrived early, even Slab and Veronica. They stood around talking quietly until the Warden arrived on the dot of 3:30 and bade them all take places round the table. English Breakfast tea brewed from real leaves was ready, so Victoria poured it out through a silver strainer. She served it to each guest in a Wedgewood China cup decorated with a blue Anthemion pattern. The table held thin-cut sandwiches of smoked salmon, cheddar cheese with chutney, and creamy tarragon chicken. Scones with Cornish clotted cream and strawberry preserve were arranged on Wedgewood China. The centerpieces were two silver three-tier cake stands, plentifully stacked with selections of raspberry pastries, lemon tartlets and chocolate, coffee, and orange gateaux.

As the Warden started the sandwich plates circulating, New England student Lawrence Everett, burst out, "This is so cool, Warden, these English afternoon teas really hit the spot. And you've managed to serve yours in a Greek setting. Do you think modern English culture today is much influenced by ancient Greek ideas?" Victoria easily recognized this as a gambit designed to win her goodwill by giving her a platform to pontificate on her favorite subject. She was far too experienced a hostess to fall for it, so she replied shortly, "Yes, certainly, Greece was the cradle of democracy, the English legal system owes much to Solon of Athens. Then, of course, science and mathematics are indebted to Euclid. Furthermore, the Socratic teaching method of questions and answers is well in evidence here at Excelsis." Immediately turning to Russell, she asked, "How ever did you manage to charm our reticent Mrs. Maggs?" All heads turned expectantly toward him.

"Ah!" he said playfully, "we'd all like to know more about the mysterious ways to ladies' hearts!" Assuming a wise expression, he continued, "I'm as puzzled as anyone, but I always praise the work she does cleaning and tidying my room, and I always laugh at her jokes. This morning, for example, she asked me, "How do bees brush their hair?" When I said, "Not a clue, how do they?" she exclaimed, "They use honeycombs!" Everyone groaned as Russell continued, "I always ask after her nephew, whom she adores, and I help her up when she falls."

Ambi asked the question on everyone's mind, "Why does she fall?"

With a twinkle in his eye, Russell said, "It's not wine or spirits, she's most abstemious. It's not vertigo, she's sound and healthy, but accidents happen in the best regulated Residences."

"What sort of accidents?" Shuchun Niu, a student from Hong Kong, inquired.

"Well," said Russell frustratingly, "another reason I'm in her good books is that I'm not one to give out ladies' secrets. If you want to know, you must ask her yourself."

Conversation became more general as the Warden invited the students to help themselves to the cakes. Russell overheard Craig Campbell asking Shuchun if she was interested in rugby football.

Shyly she replied in her hesitant English, "I not seen real match, only on TV."

Craig continued to tell her about his successes on the rugby field and then said, "You could watch me play in the match against Edinburgh at the Sports Centre tomorrow, and then we could go back to my place for a drink."

"Thank for that," she replied, "what time is match?"

He told her it was at 2:00 p.m.

South African Nthanda Nkoli was listening politely as Lawrence was telling her about the complexities of the American political system. Then Russell asked her how she liked living in the UK and listened as she said she missed the support of her large family of four brothers and two sisters.

Attention focused once more on the Warden when Veronica told her that several of them were taking Olympia Sheldrake-Smith's paleontology course. "She's evidently an atheist because she tossed a Bible on the floor in her first lecture."

"Yes," Warden Sinclair replied, "she makes that grandstand gesture every year. She would like Excelsis to promote atheism more vigorously, but Christians, of whom I am one, are not in favor."

"Oh, I think the University should," Slab interjected. "The fossils demonstrate the fact of evolution, and that tells us there is no god. Excelsis should be helping students to relax and enjoy their lives. The Bible is just another collection of folktales. Its stories of judgement and a reckoning to come are pure fiction, designed to control the simple-minded peoples of long ago. Such religious taboos are hopelessly outdated." Confidently he added, "We can do what we want. There will be no final reckoning. We don't have to follow any set of prudish rules, and we don't have to account for what we do to anyone. As long as we don't run afoul of any meddling social bodies, or get convicted of antisocial behavior, then anything goes. Evolution teaches us that we must maximize what we can get out of life. It's designed us as capsules for the preservation of selfish DNA." Russell could practically see him banging his chest as he continued, "Evolution is the engine of nature's creativity, and that means ensuring that the fittest, strongest, and best of us pass on as much of our DNA as we can. We should live life to its fullest extent without regard for any old-fashioned moral restraints. It will be good for society and good for the evolutionary future of our species."

His fervent speech produced mixed reactions among the group. Veronica and Craig looked approving, Russell appeared doubtful, and Shuchun and Nthanda's faces showed bewilderment. The Warden, Lawrence, and Ambi all had pained expressions on their faces.

"When everyone does what they think is best for themselves," Ambi finally said, "anarchy results. William Golding's novel, *Lord of the Flies*, aptly illustrates this. When societies decide their laws and conventions without reference to God, terrible consequences can happen. Think of the Nazis! Think of Pol Pot and the killing fields of Cambodia! Furthermore, if social rules are just something locally agreed upon, then when individuals encounter difficulties, or when they see some advantage, they always ignore them, just deciding that they don't apply to themselves in this instance. It eventually leads to a badly dysfunctional society! In reality, everyone agrees that such things as child abuse, rape, torture, and brutality are moral outrages, even if sanctioned by governments, cultures, or ideologies."

She looked round challengingly. "Don't you think that those who do not agree with this are abnormal and morally degenerate?" Nobody said anything. "It can't be denied that moral values exist independent of the thinking of any group of people," she continued. "Our innate sense of right and wrong offers strong evidence for the existence of objective moral values. That they originate with God is the only viable explanation."

Slab and Veronica looked annoyed. "Altruistic and moral behavior are just evolutionary adaptations. You should read what Dawkins and Dennett have to say about it," Slab snapped.

But Ambi was not intimidated. "Those purported kin selection explanations are hopelessly inadequate when it comes to accounting for the full range of human behavior. A so-called school of minimalist academics claim that much of the Bible is an imaginary history projected into the past by scribes living centuries later. That way those who want to can label scriptural morality as myth or fiction. But time and again other leading scholars have pointed out such biblical scholarship is totally driven by naturalist ideology. In fact, the minimalist approach is being more and more questioned. The findings of actual archaeology are increasingly confirming the reliability of Bible history and consequently undergird what Scripture teaches. It's only popular cultural pundits endlessly parroting last century dogma that maintain otherwise."

Seeing Slab and Veronica's reactions and sensing an argument developing, the Warden brought things to a halt by saying, "Education is the ability to listen to almost anything without losing one's temper." Looking meaningly round, she added, "I'm sure Ambi and Roger will maintain

Excelsis's reputation for excellent education?" Her offer of a glass of white wine indicated that the teatime was coming to an end.

Russell noticed that Ambi declined the wine. Having now learned her name, he wondered if "Ambi" could be a shortened form of a longer name. While what she had said was new to him, he was strangely curious to hear more. As they were all leaving the Day Room, he determined to find out more about her.

As Ambi departed with the others, she tapped Shuchun on the arm and signaled she would like to speak to her. Recognizing that the girl was shy with little experience of British culture, she led her to a quiet corner and said, "I believe Craig invited you to watch his rugby match and then come to his place for a drink?"

"Yes, that right."

"Craig's invitation was to his place, rather than to a public bar. After the match, the rugby players will all celebrate with a lot of alcohol. Things could get unpleasantly physical. A big forceful guy, Craig doesn't take well to being denied anything. I would be very wary of going away from public areas with him after the match."

"Ah, thank you. I understand. I still learning British customs. I follow your advice."

"You have a beautiful name," Ambi said. "Tell me what it means."

"My name mean 'Pure beauty,'" she replied happily, "and other name 'Niu' is simply 'girl.'"

"That name's exactly right for you. Always stay beautiful and pure!"

Just then Nthanda approached them and asked Ambi, "I think from what you were saying just now, that you're a practicing Christian?"

"That's right."

"Do you go regularly to church?"

"Yes, as often as I can. Why do you ask?"

"Could I go with you next time you go? I so miss the services and the friendship of my church back home in South Africa!"

"Of course. My church is a friendly one in the nearby town of Dunchester, and I'm planning to attend this coming weekend. We could meet up and go together. Would about 9 a.m. in the Residence vestibule suit you?"

"That would be great. I'll see you then."

Ambi went back to her room in a thoughtful mood. Printing a couple photos of her chains walk and pinning them up, she decided that she would apply for membership of the CC Club. She wanted the experience of joining in the charitable work they undertook and hoped she could make more friends among other club members. The organization admitted only about twenty new members every year, but they, together with all the life members, formed a close-knit network supporting one another. She downloaded the application form, filled in all the questions, wrote her personal statement, and sent it off.

Chapter 6. Family Failings

After the Warden's Tea, Russell's week flowed rapidly by. What Ambi had said had intrigued him. He had to agree that no matter what cultural norms approved, or what state legislation permitted, rape, torture, and child abuse were still despicable crimes. Equally, love, gratitude, kindness, altruism were undeniably good qualities. But surely evolution had a good explanation of how such behaviors emerged in humanity. Online, he found evolutionary explanations attributing human aggression to the need for survival as well as reproductive potential. But such speculative concepts seemed rather weak to him. They didn't explain why certain behaviors were universally regarded as wrong, if not evil, and why those who did them deserved punishment. If such violent and aggressive actions helped evolutionary "progress," why would anyone feel the need to condemn them? He thought the evolution-inspired theory of Kin Selection might account for some altruistic behavior, but hardly for all the self-sacrificing deeds people would do for what were otherwise total strangers. Furthermore, Kin Selection did nothing to rationalize why society regarded kindness and altruism universally as "good" and "right." As for Ambi's discussion about archaeology and the Bible, surely it was just fundamentalist moonshine! Everyone knew the Bible was a mass of errors and fantastic stories.

By Friday, it had been two weeks since he had met with Sir George Faircross to suggest expanding his research topic to include his *longiferase* project. But he had still heard nothing from him. Had the man forgotten? Or had he concluded the expensive extra resources were unjustified?

That morning his father, Karl Marshall, had texted him, asking him to come home, because he was worried about Melanie, Russell's older sister. Determined to go home that weekend, he decided that if he had still heard nothing from Sir George by Monday, he would set up another meeting with him. He texted his father saying to expect him home that evening.

Russell's home was in the nearby town of Dunchester. At one time Karl had worked in shipbuilding but lost his job when the local shipyards couldn't compete with those in the Far East. The attitude of the government and of his employers had embittered his already socialist and atheist outlook. Eventually he teamed up with a friend to start a construction business. At first, they had just taken on loft conversions and conservatories, but the company steadily expanded to house building and eventually large contracts. By the time Russell and his sister Melanie were teenagers, Karl was joint proprietor of a fairly prosperous operation.

Melanie was a year older than Russell. The two had grown up in an atmosphere of crusading anti-capitalism. While they were still young, their father had read aloud during meals and in the evenings from the writings of eminent socialists and thinkers such as Bertrand Russell, Karl Marx, Rosa Luxemburg, and George Orwell. Continually bombarded with Karl's socialist and atheist rhetoric, brother and sister clung to one another during his rages against governments and politicians who ran counter to his ideas. From an early age he took them to political rallies and to meetings of SOPYS, the sceptics society Karl had helped to found. As a result, Russell had grown up thinking religion was little more than priestcraft, hypocrisy, and money making. Hardly ever having been inside a church, he imagined that all clergy were either like the ranting TV evangelists, or like the richly robed priests of establishment and orthodox churches.

Russell and Melanie had always been close. He had protected her from bullying at school, and she had sometimes shouldered the blame for his escapades at home. Karl employed both of them in his construction work during school and other holidays, so they both had good knowledge of the building trade. His father had hoped his son would join him in the business and was greatly disappointed when Russell finally opted for a career in biochemistry.

Though Karl had been a heavy smoker, after a long struggle he had managed to quit. Unfortunately, he hadn't succeeded early enough. His wife contracted cancer from the constant cigarette smoke in their home and died when Russell and Melanie were in their mid-teens.

Losing her mother had deeply affected Melanie, causing her gradually to lose interest in life. Even though she eventually went to a large Midlands University to study political science, it only accentuated her downward spiral. Her father's oft repeated quotation that "we are only organized mud" ingrained itself in her mind. She could see nothing ahead of her except suffering, struggle, and death. Her mother's painful passing made her expect the same for herself. Existence was a pointless struggle toward the grave. What was the point in striving when everyone was doomed to become part of the food chain sooner or later? Melanie had been a beautiful and clever girl, but now more and more neglected her health and appearance. She couldn't be bothered with learning, and gradually found herself needing more and more alcohol to get through the day. On completing her degree, she had obtained a job in local government, but her attitude, absences, and careless mistakes led to her dismissal. Now she lived at home where Karl expected her to keep house and help him on the clerical side of his business.

Aware of Melanie's dismal housekeeping, Russell picked up a bag of groceries before catching the bus home to Dunchester. Their father had built a substantial modern home for himself and his family in an upscale suburb of the city. The entrance way and cloakroom opened onto a central hall, with an impressive stairway of alternating dark and light wood steps, flanked by a fretted balustrade leading to a gallery and an upper level. On the ground floor, white oak doors with Rennie Mackintosh glazed panels led to a drawing room, a games room, a library-cum-office, a dining room, and a kitchen. Five bedrooms and a storeroom occupied the upper-level gallery.

That evening Russell rang the doorbell to announce his arrival before letting himself in. Melanie came into the hallway holding a glass of gin in her hand, but she put it down as he gave her a warm hug and kissed her cheek, declaring, "It's so good to see you again!" As they went into the untidy drawing room, he began to tell her all his news and asked about what she had been doing lately. Her apathetic replies and unkempt appearance saddened him. After dumping his stuff in his bedroom, he came down and coerced Melanie into helping as he began to prepare a meal with the food he'd brought with him. After a while Karl arrived home and Melanie seemed to brighten up a bit.

Later that evening she went out, announcing she had a date. "She's probably gone to a pub she frequents in the city center," Karl remarked. He told Russell how worried he was about her, how depressed she seemed, how poor her work habits were, and that she was drinking far too much. Both wondered what on earth they could do to help her. They talked far into the evening, Karl updating Russell on the steady success of his business, and

Russell describing his life at the University. When 11:00 p.m. came and Melanie still hadn't returned, they began to worry. By 1:00 a.m. they were seriously concerned. They knew she would have missed the last bus, and taxis were hard to find in Dunchester at that time of night.

Just as Russell was suggesting they take the car and start scouring the streets, the doorbell rang. He opened the door to find a man and a girl supporting a groggy-looking Melanie. Hurriedly he took Melanie from them, at the same time inviting them in. "I feel sick," Melanie said in a choked voice. Russell led her to the bathroom and helped her kneel beside the lavatory as her stomach violently voided itself. Wiping her face, he half carried her up to her room and settled her onto her bed where, muttering, she fell asleep.

Karl had ushered the two individuals who had brought Melanie home into the drawing room and was talking to them as Russell entered. To his amazement he realized that the girl was Ambi, and her astonished expression showed she was just as dumbfounded to see him.

Seeing their faces Karl asked, "Do you two know each other?"

Recovering his composure, Russell said, "In a way we do. This is Ambi, an undergraduate living in Benedict Hall where I'm a sub-warden."

"I had no idea you even lived in Dunchester," she exclaimed, sounding embarrassed. "This is Daniel Smith, a friend of mine from church."

Just then Daniel interrupted her. "The church runs a Hope Food Share program. Late most Friday evenings we take a van into Dunchester with soup and sandwiches for the homeless living on the streets. Tonight, we came across this young lady stumbling down the main street. We suspected she'd had too much to drink. A car with four men inside was crawling along not far behind her. Afraid for her safety, we approached her and asked if she would like a lift home. At first, she angrily refused, saying she could look after herself, but she seemed on the point of passing out and was leaning on a lamp post."

"Yes," Ambi continued, "she was pretty helpless, so we checked in her handbag, found this address, and brought her here. We had no idea you lived here," she said, glancing at Russell.

"Melanie's my sister," he explained. "She's going through a bad patch personally and is drinking too much. We're extremely grateful to you for bringing her home safely. I can't thank you enough for your kindness! We were terribly worried and on the point of setting out to look for her."

Karl added his sincere thanks before asking them what the Hope Food Share program was. Ambi explained it was one of her church's community assistance projects. Members and friends donated money and food. Supermarkets also supplied food items from surplus and unsold stock. The church organized distribution to needy families and once a week ran a van to the town center with items for the homeless. Russell felt a bit ashamed as his father asked, "What does the church make out of it?"

With a wry look, Daniel replied, "It's all run by unpaid volunteers and from voluntary contributions. There's no charge for anything."

"Many of the homeless have problems of one kind and another," Ambi added. "For those who are interested and will listen, we offer free advice on how to stop smoking, how to get their finances in order, or how to break the downward spiral into alcoholism."

Despite Karl's hostility to anything connected with religion, both he and Russell were interested in what she said. "What do you recommend for the alcoholics?" Russell asked.

"Well," Ambi said, "there is the local branch of Alcoholics Anonymous, but for those who can take time off from work and are suffering from depression or other underlying health problems, we suggest they register for a one-month residential course at Fidem Health and Wellbeing Institute. There is a reasonable charge for meals and accommodation," she added, looking at Karl with a twinkle. "They have a comparatively high success rate, but there are no guarantees of course."

"Yes," Daniel added, "they employ a holistic approach and try to address physical, mental, and spiritual problems as well as alcohol addiction."

Ambi wearily suggested that it was time they were getting home. Both Russell and Karl thanked them again, and Russell offered to drive them home, but Daniel explained they still had the van parked outside and that he would see Ambi home.

As they were leaving, Russell said to Ambi, "I was very interested in what you said the other day at the Warden's Tea. I'd like to hear more on that. Could we meet over a drink in the Bishop's Arms?"

"OK, that would be nice, when do you suggest?"

"Would Monday at around 6:00 p.m. be OK?"

"Yes, I'll see you then."

Russell ushered them to the door and looked curiously at their van. It was a large, battered Ford Transit type with "Hope Food Share" painted on the side. *It's a good thing all the neighbors are asleep, or they would have seen the van and begun gossiping that my father's business has gone bankrupt and we were living on the breadline!* he thought to himself.

"That's a beautiful and kind-hearted girl." Karl remarked as they both went to check on Melanie. "It's a pity she's mixed up with those benighted Christians. Otherwise, if I were a young man again, I'd be after her." His son recognized it as a hint he should be looking for a nice girl to settle down with. He had to agree with his father about Ambi's attractiveness, but he thought, *you have no idea of her fundamentalist beliefs!* Melanie was deeply asleep, so they made sure she was properly covered and then turned in themselves.

Meanwhile, as he drove her home, Daniel was telling Ambi that she shouldn't be so ready to meet young men in pubs. "Watch out he doesn't take any liberties with you." But she was too tired to bother answering. She just sat with her eyes closed, thinking how absurd to talk about taking liberties in a public bar and how old-fashioned and controlling Daniel was. The next morning, she remembered that she had promised to meet Nthanda in the Benedict Hall vestibule. Instead, she texted her to tell her which bus to catch to Dunchester and promised to meet her there at the bus station.

When Melanie woke up the next day, her head throbbed excruciatingly. Unable to face breakfast when she eventually got up, she sat wincing at every noise and snapping at Russell and Karl. Russell wanted to tell her gently to go easy on the alcohol. To warn her of the damage she was doing to her liver and of the danger she was putting herself in. But he could see it wasn't the right moment, so he satisfied himself with offering her cups of strong coffee. Then he and his father retired to the study, leaving her in peace in the drawing room, and talked over what they could do to help her.

They both doubted Alcoholics Anonymous was the answer. Her problem was not just alcohol, it was a more deep-seated mental one. She saw herself as worthless, had come to see her existence as just a brief flicker, a mere eddy of consciousness in the impersonal evolutionary struggle. "Maybe a visit to a health spa or a wellness retreat might do her some good," Russell mused out loud.

"I'd do anything to try to help her," his father said. "We'll see how she is after the weekend. Maybe this experience will shock her out of her depression a bit. Meanwhile I'll check out the internet to see what's available in terms of health spas."

Chapter 7. **Tavern Tête-à-Tête**

THE SUB-WARDENS OF BENEDICT Hall had a rotating system to ensure that one of them was always on hand to deal with any student problems. Russell returned to Columburgh on Sunday in time for his duty at the Residence evening meal. Then, early the next morning, he greeted Mrs. Maggs on his way to breakfast and laughed heartily as she said, "I know they say money talks, but all mine ever says is 'goodbye'!" Arriving at his lab, he gave Melanie a quick ring to make sure she was OK. Then, opening his laptop, he trawled past a notice he had won ten million dollars on a postcode lottery, dumped a unique business offer from the ex-wife of an African dictator, and ignored an invitation to register for a world congress on trends in pharmaceutical toxicology for only $1,500. But he was surprised to see an email from a company called MoliMart in his inbox.

He knew a little about the company. It was a subsidiary of a huge American pharmaceutical group. Sir George was a scientific consultant for them. Russell was fairly certain Faircross also owned shares in the company. They operated a research and development facility in a former manor house not far from Dunchester that had been converted, enlarged, and greatly extended. The company had renamed it Pleasant Park, but the place had a sinister reputation and locals still called it by its original name of Bleak End. His father had done construction work there as part of their expansion and, during holiday jobs with his father, he had been to the site regularly. The company made most of its money from selling test kits for various infections, slimming aids, tonics, nicotine alternatives, hair loss preventives, and other health and beauty products.

The email was an invitation from Human Resources at MoliMart for him to come for an interview at 11:00 a.m. the very next day at Pleasant Park, travel expenses to be reimbursed. It surprised Russell to receive the

35

offer, because he had no connection with them and hadn't applied for an interview. He surmised it had something to do with Sir George and immediately emailed his acceptance. Russell worked on his research project during the day and chatted with Zemki who had been very friendly during the past few days. Then he went to the gym for his regular workout, showered, and returned to the lab. Later, he walked to the Bishop's Arms in good time to meet Ambi.

When she arrived, Russell noticed that while she wore no jewelry and little if any makeup, she had a fresh attractiveness that caught the attention of the other men in the room. Her luxurious chestnut-brown curls helped not a little. After he offered her a drink, he went to the bar to get the apple juice that she asked for and a half pint for himself. They found seats in a quiet corner and surveyed one another quizzically. Russell had been revising the initial dislike he had taken to her. Hardly the pig-headed, doctrinaire, half-wit he had thought all creationists must be, she was actually intelligent, articulate, and well-informed, even if she had wrong ideas about some things. Recognizing that she must be super-busy on her degree course, it had astonished him to discover she still found time to distribute food to the homeless. Helping Melanie had made a deep impression on him. "Thanks for coming along," he said. "I hope this isn't interrupting your schedule too much?"

"Oh, it's no trouble. I'm fairly up to date with my courses. How is Melanie? Did she recover OK?"

"She had a terrible hangover the next day but doesn't seem to have suffered any serious physical harm. She just needs to get her mind back in order."

"Perhaps she needs a new hairstyle. I've known a change of style to completely transform a girl's outlook."

Russell smiled, but he looked doubtful as he said, "I'll suggest it to her, but she doesn't care about her appearance. I suspect the problem is deeper seated. She needs to change the inside of her head more than the outside." Changing tack, he asked, "you said some intriguing things at the Warden's Tea the other day. Were you really serious in claiming that the stories and accounts in the Bible are reliable history? What did you mean by minimalist critics?"

Ambi's expression was serious as she said, "You know how this is an age of fake news, fake information, and fake science? The internet is awash with conspiracy theories, photoshopped pictures, made-up quotes, and propaganda. Nowhere is there more misinformation and outright lies than in the area of biblical and religious subjects. Minimalists belong to a so-called liberal wing of biblical criticism that treats the Bible as seriously unreliable in almost every way. For them it's fiction, fraud, and fantasy. Their dismissals of Bible narratives, and their skeptical reconstructions of Jewish history, have caught the attention of the sensation-hungry media. They make a big impact on naive sections of the public."

"How do you mean?"

"Well, take Jesus for example. Media pundits often claim He never existed. At a recent lecture, when this claim was made it led to a round of applause," she said disgustedly.

Russell nodded, having himself heard similar claims several times from speakers at the Sceptics Society.

"The reality is quite the opposite," Ambi said earnestly. "The non-Christian Roman historian Tacitus, and the Jewish historian Josephus both mention Jesus' crucifixion. Furthermore, Roman officials Suetonius and Pliny the Younger both expressed their contempt of Christians in their writings from around the first century A.D. More than 100 very early manuscripts have references to Jesus' life, written by Christians in the first two centuries A.D. Far more evidence about Jesus has survived than about the works of the historians Herodotus, Thucydides, or Livy. More is reliably known about Jesus and His life than for almost any other individual from ancient times, even including Roman emperors. All serious historians accept that Jesus was a real person who lived and taught in Palestine and was crucified by Pontius Pilate."

"How do you know all this stuff?"

"My father is a theologian who still authors articles for Christian periodicals, although now he is the pastor of a couple conservative Christian congregations. I've often helped him check his articles and prepare his sermons."

"Sermons! Aren't they the most boring affairs in the world? They say that a good sermon should have a good beginning and a good ending. And they should be as close together as possible," Russell said with a smile.

Ambi laughed. "It depends on which church you go to and who is preaching. Modern preachers know they have to compete with the media. Nowadays preachers screen PowerPoints, tell stories, and even make jokes. Sermons can be informative, interesting—and even entertaining."

Slab, Veronica, Nollum, Anna, and others had arrived and were standing by the bar talking. Veronica came over and stood close to Russell. "What secrets are you two sharing over here?"

"We're talking about minimalist critics and biblical history," Russell retorted.

Veronica grimaced, then tossed her blonde mane. Fluttering her eyelashes, she said, "Surely there are more tempting things around here to pay attention to?"

"This is a serious conversation about weighty issues."

"Yeah, it's always like that with Ambi. I've got more frivolous things to do."

"Meow, meow!" Russell said with a grin. "You'll be growing whiskers if you don't watch out!"

"I can purr, if I'm treated nicely!"

"I'm a dog lover myself."

Veronica walked away, swaying her hips. *She's a girl who likes to be noticed, and seeks admiration from every male she meets,* Russell thought to himself. *I've never seen Ambi peacocking for male attention. She's interested in gaining knowledge and making the world a better place.* Shrugging, he turned to Ambi and caught an amused expression on her face.

"A penny for them?" she said.

"Just trying for some insights into the female psyche."

"What did you find there?"

"Some Aladdin's caves and some chambers of horrors! Girls may be either seraphs or serpents, but it's mind-bending deciding which is which!"

"Oh, I'm definitely a seraph!"

"Sure, you look most seraphic," he replied teasingly. "But for all I know you might be a fallen seraph! Seriously though, what makes you think we should take the Jewish folk tales in the Bible as real history?"

"Archaeology from the Holy Land has backed up or shed light on Bible history on countless occasions. It's not too much to say that archaeology has been overwhelmingly successful in confirming Bible truth. But don't just take my word for it," Ambi added. "Read books by genuine experts like Craig Blomberg and Kenneth Kitchen. I'll email you the details if you're interested. By all means check out what the minimalists say as well but be aware that their skeptical theories have shown up wrong again and again as new archaeological discoveries have overturned them. Their sloppy scholarship has come under strong fire. One critic even labelled their writings sociological poppycock! There is compelling evidence the Bible records are true and often perhaps eyewitness accounts. It's a great pity popular pundits and the media ignore this."

"You're a persuasive defender of Bible knowledge!" he said, again with a smile. "I would definitely like to follow up on it. Please do email me details of those books." Suddenly he glanced at his watch. "Look at the time! We shouldn't be late for dinner at Benedict Hall." They got up and made their way to the Residence. Although Russell would have liked to ask what her relationship with Daniel was, he didn't want to pry into her personal affairs at their first face-to-face meeting.

Chapter 8. **Betrayed**

THE NEXT DAY STARTED fine with a hint of Indian summer, as Russell dressed carefully in a dark suit and patterned tie. He checked out the MoliMart website to see what the company claimed for itself. They seemed to be a profitable outfit with a market capitalization in the £100M bracket and a steady share price. Their website made all the usual upbeat statements about their concerns for the environment and a diverse workforce. He ordered a taxi to take him the fifteen or so miles and, as he rode along, jotted down a few questions to ask at the interview. The sky clouded over during the trip, and drizzle started as the taxi deposited him outside the high security main gatehouse of Pleasant Park. Cameras pivoted as he pushed through a narrow turnstile into a small reception area. After asking his business, the duty security officer had Russell sign his name and time of arrival, before phoning through to ask for instructions. After a short wait, another security officer escorted him along a path to the new part of the complex. Russell could hear guard dogs baying in the distance. He was shown to a reception area and offered a coffee by a pleasant young woman. "They'll be ready for you in just a few minutes," she said.

On the dot of 11:00 a.m. a message evidently arrived on her computer, because she beckoned Russell over and escorted him up a flight of stairs to a modern reception room. It contained no-nonsense IKEA type furniture and had pictures of MoliMart factories and company directors on the walls. A man and a woman sized Russell up as he entered and took a seat facing them across the pine table. They didn't offer to shake hands, but the man said he was head of Human Resources and introduced the woman as "Dr. Irma Vonvoigt, Director of Innovative Research." The HR manager spoke for about 10 minutes telling Russell much that he already knew from their website. He claimed that though their balance sheet was important, MoliMart's aim was to bring improvements to the health and wellbeing of society. "Our products and services," he said, "are all chosen, priced, and tailored to enhance the safety, security, and living conditions of the public. MoliMart manufacturing and research is modern, progressive, and designed to protect the environment. MoliMart is a benevolent employer with a deep commitment to worker health and welfare. Furthermore, we are always striving to attain as diverse a workforce as possible."

In Dr. Vonvoigt, Russell saw a solid-looking individual with neat iron-grey hair above a secretive fleshy face with thin humorless lips. Her name and appearance suggested a foreign origin, but she spoke perfect English. "MoliMart conducts research into a wide variety of health-related areas but, several years ago, we started a program designed to investigate human longevity," she told Russell. "Sir George Faircross is one of our consultants, and at a recent board meeting he explained his ground-breaking ideas based around the *longiferase* enzyme. We decided to buy into his *telomerase* program and devote significant resources to this research." Eying Russell, she said, "I believe Sir George already briefed you on his ideas and that you are familiar with the basics of his project?"

The realization that Faircross had in effect betrayed him came as a rude shock to Russell. His supervisor had unscrupulously adopted the project as his own and sold it to MoliMart. Feeling extremely uncomfortable and let down, he realized that it would do no good protesting that the idea was his. A student's word would not carry any weight against that of the eminent Sir George. Suddenly he thought back to Slab's comment about evolution teaching that everyone must maximize what they get out of life without regard to moral restraints. That the atheist Faircross operated along the same principles now dawned on Russell. An opportunity to enhance his personal reputation had been presented to him, and he had seized it without regard for someone lower in the academic scale. Realizing that there was little he could do just then, Russell just nodded rather blankly.

Sir George, Dr Irma continued, had recommended him to them as someone familiar with the *telomerase* background who was also an expert with protein visualization software. MoliMart had arranged to act as partners in the project. They would provide technical resources and supplies as well as analytical and spectroscopic services. Dr. Zemki Illovian had been offered a job at MoliMart and would transfer there during the coming weeks as he wound down his research at Excelsis. She said the plan was for her to become co-supervisor with Sir George of Russell's doctoral research. He would continue with his end of the project at Excelsis but would spend time each week at MoliMart with Zemki and the lab technical officers. The company would increase Russell's maintenance grant by 15 percent, and they would guarantee him a job for at least four years when he graduated with his Ph.D. She invited Russell to accept the arrangement and sign a contract.

He felt helpless. If he refused, the project would anyway go ahead without him, and he would lose all the excitement of being part of a fascinating new science to which he had opened the door. Probably he would have to leave Sir George's research group, losing all the work he had done so far, and then have to start again with another supervisor on a different project. It was a daunting prospect. When he asked Dr. Irma what Sir George's role would be, she told him he would become a member of MoliMart's Board of Directors but would also continue with his professorial duties at Excelsis. Russell could see there would be major financial rewards for Sir George, along with the prestige of his association with MoliMart. Not only would he receive substantial remuneration as a director, but if the project worked out well, his shares in the company would ensure he raked in more dividends.

Russell felt the deal was highly unfair to him. For just a few hundred pounds a year, MoliMart obtained possession of a project potentially worth multiple millions. He asked Vonvoigt who would hold the intellectual property rights to the research and she told him it would be MoliMart. Then he asked about the publication of his thesis. She explained that he could write and defend it, but it would remain sequestered from the public until the company had obtained patent protection for any products or procedures developed. In the same way, publication of his work in science periodicals would have to wait. Lack or delay of publications would seriously damage his chances of getting a job with any other employer when he finished his Ph.D. When he pointed it out to her and inquired if MoliMart's remuneration package included the issue of shares each year to company employees, the HR man told him it did, but that he wouldn't qualify for any until he became full-time staff.

Russell said the benefits to him seemed slight, and he would have the added expense of travelling to Pleasant Park every week. It appeared that MoliMart put little value on his input to the project. Dr. Irma warmed up a little and said perhaps they could increase his grant by 20 percent and give him the use of a company car. "Not to worry," she said, "because you are assured of a job at MoliMart once you obtain your Ph.D." A cursory glance at the contract they showed him included a non-disclosure agreement and was provisional for one year, subject to satisfactory progress. When he stated that he would like to take the document with him and talk it over with Sir George before deciding, they reluctantly agreed, provided he came to a decision within a week. With that the interview ended. Escorted back to the reception area, Russell asked the receptionist to call him a taxi. Rain steadily descended from a gray sky as he travelled back to his lab. Russell felt perplexed and disillusioned. Back at the lab, he emailed Sir George and asked for an appointment to see him as soon as possible.

He was in a gloomy mood the next morning as he greeted Mrs. Maggs on his way down to breakfast. Because he forgot to ask her about her nephew, Arthur, and, sensing his mood, she quoted, "Merry music gladdens the heart and taxing toil makes the blues depart!" Her parting shot was, "Don't forget your workout today." Sir George had emailed back, setting 9:00 a.m. as the time to meet. As Russell made his way to the lab, he thought about what to say to him. He took the lift up to Faircross' office where his secretary admitted him. "I expect you've come to discuss the offer MoliMart have made you," Sir George began.

"Yes, that's right, but why did you claim it was your idea! I outlined the project to you in our discussion two weeks ago."

Sir George remained completely unperturbed. "Your memory of the occasion seems at odds with mine. Certainly, you made an important suggestion, but the complete concept was mine. You should be grateful to me for arranging with MoliMart to supply the needed resources and offering you an advantageous contract with the prospect of a permanent job at the end. In any case, you can rely on me to give you the credit you deserve when it comes to the publication of this research in the learned journals."

Russell now doubted if Faircross would give him recognition at any stage, but, realizing his other options meant starting again at square one, he decided he'd try to make the best of the situation. He showed Sir George the MoliMart contract and asked his advice. Faircross recommended he definitely insist on the 20 percent grant supplement, and suggested he also ask for an allowance toward the fuel, insurance, and maintenance of the company car. He further said the contract should guarantee that the permanent job with MoliMart start on acceptance of his Ph.D. thesis rather than on the date of his graduation. Russell left feeling somewhat mollified. Although he had lost control of the *telomerase* project, he was still master of the visualization software he had developed. It had been the essential aid to his discovery of the concept. Well aware how easily computers could get stolen or hacked, as a matter of self-preservation when he got back to his lab, he introduced further security measures to his visualization software app, including revolving passwords and his fingerprint.

Afterward, he found an email from Ambi in his inbox with details of the books she had mentioned. In case the authors were Bible thumping pastors from cow colleges in the American Bible Belt, he checked them out on the internet. Finding they were highly regarded academics who had authored many serious works, he ordered Craig Blomberg's *Can We Still Believe the Bible* from Amazon and borrowed Kenneth Kitchen's *On the Reliability of the Old Testament* from the University library.

Chapter 9. **Tangling with Trees**

ON WEDNESDAY RUSSELL RETURNED the MoliMart contract to Dr. Irma, writing to ask her to slot in the changes that Sir George had suggested. Later, he headed over to Prof. Olympia's lecture. Indian summer had returned. The air was mild as the sun broke through the clouds from time to time. Russell was especially fond of the flowers growing along the way. He noticed that the dog roses outside Benedict Hall were past their best and large red rose hips were growing on the rose bushes. Daisies still dappled the lawns, yellow dandelions sprinkled the verges, and groups of red poppies sprang from crannies in walls and pavements. His spirits lifted as he took in the yellows, glorious russets, and browns of the trees. In the distance, bracken and pine clothed the hillsides with a patchwork effect.

Prof. Olympia's subject that day was the phylogenetic Tree of Life. She explained that it was a branching diagram of the evolutionary relationships between all living and extinct organisms. Scientists had derived it from detailed comparisons of their shapes and anatomies. The French biologists Augier and Lamarck had proposed some of the early diagrams, but Olympia said that the best-known example was the sketch Charles Darwin had made in his notebook in 1837. A minor disturbance erupted among the students near Veronica as she was whispering about her own tattooed Tree of Life. Ignoring it, Olympia continued to show graphics depicting various ways of representing the tree. She explained that each node in the tree was called a "taxonomic unit" that represented the most recent common ancestor of various species. Surprisingly, she added that they could not be directly observed. "Such trees are extremely useful in various fields of biology, paleontology, and systematics. The edge lengths of the trees can be useful for time estimates. All life on Earth is part of a single tree which indicates our common ancestry," she emphasized.

At this point Ambi raised her hand to ask a question. A section of the class liked Ambi's questions, because they gave a break from note taking. But the majority disliked interruptions, so a discontented mutter broke out. Olympia looked annoyed but signaled for Ambi to go ahead.

"A substantial number of 'molecular trees' have been obtained recently by gene sequencing methods. Many of them, particularly those for microorganisms, disagree with the classic anatomical tree. Scientists have been talking about forests of trees, or nets of relationships. Wouldn't you agree that this calls into question the concept of common ancestry?"

Olympia's annoyed expression deepened. "There have been a few apparent discrepancies and puzzles raised by the molecular trees, but they will soon be sorted out as science progresses. The anatomical Tree of Life is a fabulous achievement of paleontology. There is no doubt whatsoever about the common ancestry of all living things." She resumed her lecture, illustrating sections of the tree relating to various biological families, orders, and classes.

Russell emerged from the lecture theater still thinking about Ambi's question. If scientists really did have doubts about the phylogenetic tree, and common ancestry, it would be a huge difficulty for evolution itself. Careful study was needed. He joined the stream of students heading to the common room where a group had collected round Slab and Veronica. She had pulled up her top and was displaying the Tree of Life tattoo on her side to an admiring group of males. "This puts me right at the top of the evolutionary tree. In me you behold evolution's most perfect production!" She repeated it several times.

"Yeah, evolution produces some great masterworks," Slab smirked. "And some duds like that tiresome creationist birdbrain. She ought to be silenced."

Russell joined the group. "It doesn't sound like she's firing duds," he observed. "Olympia looked quite rattled for a moment. Ambi asks intelligent questions that deserve better answers than she's getting."

"All those creationist objections have been refuted and double refuted long ago. She's wasting the class's time," Slab growled impatiently.

"So, what's the refutation of her statements about Molecular Trees? Olympia didn't seem to know. She just fell back on an assertion. I'm beginning to think she isn't giving us the full or honest picture." Lawrence, the New Englander, and Shuchun nodded in agreement.

"Are you one of those creationist boneheads, too? I don't have time to waste bandying words with ignorant airheads," Slab said as he swaggered away with Nollum, Craig, and his judo buddies. Veronica gave Russell a rueful look, perhaps meant to soften Slab's rudeness, but she and Anna followed him.

On the lawn outside Benedict Hall, students were practicing dances in the pleasant sunshine for the forthcoming Autumn Ball. Their expressions showed their happiness as they crossed arms, spun one another around, advanced and retired. Russell noticed Ambi and her friend Sarah McBride had made themselves daisy chains and were joining in. The Autumn Ball was scheduled for next Sunday, and he decided to buy a couple tickets, although he knew choosing who to take with him would be a problem.

He was busy during the next few days, getting his research into shape. A new contract arrived from MoliMart that included all the extras he had requested. He wondered then if he should have asked for more, but signed it anyway, and sent it back. It was due to come into force in a couple weeks. Russell was eager to know when he could claim the car and what make and model it would be.

On Friday, a message arrived in his inbox from the membership secretary of the CC Club. It contained a list of 33 new applicants, with their personal statements appended, that had been circulated to all current CC Club members. They were invited to vote for those who deserved the honor, and blackball unsuitable ones. Slab and Veronica were on the list and so was Ambi, although her name had an asterisk beside it. He was intrigued to find that her full name was Ambrosine Amhurst. The unsigned footnote corresponding to her name read, "Belongs to a fundamentalist Christian sect. Has outdated and bigoted beliefs that are anti-science. Would lower the prestige of the club. Not considered to be suitable material for the CC Club."

Ambi was the only candidate with such a negative statement against her. Russell thought it was both untrue and very unfair. What could he do since it had already gone out to all club members? Quickly he sent an email to the membership secretary protesting the singling out of one candidate in such a manner. A reply came back apologizing and saying the footnote hadn't been approved by the whole committee and they weren't sure how it had got in. However, the damage was done.

Russell knew no Greek, but he had an idea that the name Ambrose referred to "food of the gods." Ambrosine was an unusual name, so he googled it and learned that it meant "immortal." Although not in the least superstitious, he was still struck by the coincidence. His research was a quest for longevity, and now, a girl he found interesting had the name "Immortal." Was he really attracted to her? he asked himself. She was obviously a committed Christian with religious views diametrically opposed to what he had always believed. But he had to acknowledge that he was fast coming to admire her personality and did find her attractive.

He decided that as an antidote he would try someone the opposite. Once he had dated a coed by the name of Goldie Gibson. She was only a slight acquaintance, but he knew she was a streetwise blonde in her third year. On impulse he texted her an invitation to the Benedict Autumn Ball and received a reply later in the day accepting it.

His father had asked him to come home again that weekend, because Melanie was no better. He wanted Russell to join him in persuading Melanie to enter an addiction program. On Saturday Russell travelled home. Their father took him and Melanie out for lunch. They avoided pubs to save Melanie from the temptation of alcohol, going instead to the Marine Magic restaurant. Karl ordered their famous fish and chips, Russell chose sea bass with citrus salsa, and Melanie lemon garlic butter salmon. The food was well cooked and tastefully presented, putting them all in a good mood. Back at home, father and son prepared coffee and joined Melanie in the drawing room. Karl looked fondly at his daughter and said they were really worried about her apathy and heavy drinking. Although she frowned impatiently, she continued to listen as he said, "You're my only daughter, I would be heartbroken if anything happened to you. You can't go on the way you are without seriously damaging your health."

"Alcohol only gives you a brief period of escape," Russell added. "As soon as you sober up, you slip back into your depression. What's more, while you're under the influence, you might do dangerous things or succumb to predatory males."

"I'm OK! You're exaggerating. I just like to party with friends and have a few drinks."

"Things have gone way beyond that!" her father protested. "But it's your reckless and unhappy outlook that's bothering us more than anything." Looking earnestly at her, Karl said, "Russell and I would like you to have a complete change from your regular haunts here in Dunchester. There are some really attractive health spas that offer help with out-of-control drinking habits, as well as implementing a healthful lifestyle. I've been online, and I think I've found one that would be good for you. It's called Fidem Health and Wellbeing Institute, and it's in a beautiful part of North Wales. Here is the brochure they sent me describing their programs." Russell urged her to look it over.

Deep down Melanie was unhappy with her life, but she couldn't see any way forward. It was all pointless anyway. She took it, flipping through the colorful pictures and reading the descriptions. "It's probably all hype. You can't trust what they show in these brochures."

Karl and Russell felt encouraged that at least she hadn't rejected the idea outright. "What have you got to lose? Let's look the place over on Google maps." They brought up the satellite view, and Melanie had to admit the place was housed in an attractive mansion on well-kept grounds and that the surrounding countryside was stunning. "At the very least, you could look on it as a welcome holiday. Let's give them a ring and see if they can take you? If you can't stand it, you can always phone home, and I'll come fetch you."

"Oh well, since you're so set on it, I may as well give it a try." Before she could change her mind, Karl contacted Fidem and learned they could accept her in two weeks' time. He immediately booked her for a month's stay. "I'll drive you there," he said. "You'll have your mobile phone. That way you can ring me right away if there are any problems."

"I'm sure this is the right thing for you," Russell agreed. "Father's business can manage without you for a while. You'll have a change of scene, a change of company, and experience a different way of life." Melanie looked unconvinced but felt she had run out of options. She was indifferent to what happened to her anyway, and at least she would be keeping Karl and Russell from nagging her.

To keep her occupied, Russell took Melanie to a concert of classical music by the Dunchester Musical Ensemble that evening. Afterward, he buttonholed his father and described what had happened between him, Faircross, and MoliMart. Furious, Karl wanted to phone Sir George, whom he knew from the SOPYS Society meetings, to protest about the shabby treatment of his son. Russell dissuaded him by explaining that if he fell out with Sir George, he would have to change supervisors and start his Ph.D. program again at square one. "I'm going to see how things work out with MoliMart for two or three months," he explained. "I can always fall back on a re-start as a last resort."

Chapter 10. **Benedict Hall Autumn Ball**

RUSSELL RETURNED TO COLUMBURGH the next day in good time for the Ball. He bought Goldie a wrist corsage of yellow ribbons, set with feathery green leaves. The overnight Ball would take place in the Benedict Main Hall, its adjoining rooms, and in large marquees erected for the purpose on the lawn outside. To reflect the theme of Pumpkin Phantasy, yellow and orange foliage, orange balloons, and hundreds of carved pumpkins lavishly decorated the venue. Fortunately, the fine weather held out.

Russell donned a dark blue dinner suit over a dress shirt with a black bow tie. When he knocked on the door of Goldie's room, he heard her shout for him to come in and that she would be ready in a few minutes. Her room was decorated with large photos of her posing on sunny beaches in bikinis. She emerged from the bedroom wearing a figure-hugging red, backless dress. Shear stockings, a gold mesh belt, and red high heeled shoes set off her shapely figure. Her blond curls, braided at the back, fell to her shoulders. Gold hoop earrings dangled from her ears. The fake tan, scarlet lipstick, and plucked eyebrows hinted that she had spent hours at a beauty parlor. She looked critically at the corsage Russell gave her, saying, "My last boyfriend was a jerk. He wouldn't take me shopping, though I asked him many times, but he did at least give me jewelry for the Ball." Still, she held out her arm for Russell to attach the corsage as they exchanged small talk.

"You're in biochemistry, aren't you? Isn't that dreadfully boring, and the salaries are peanuts! You should switch into management or law."

"Depends on what your interests are and how far you rise up the ladder." Russell was already having doubts about his date as they made their way down to the venue. He had purchased the more expensive tickets that included a three-course meal. They queued at the buffet, and Goldie chose cheese Quesada with salsa hors d'oeuvres, a platter with deli style roast beef, ham, turkey, and salad, with tiramisu to follow. Not satisfied with the white wine, Goldie insisted that he buy a bottle of champagne at the bar to accompany the meal.

As they found seats, she was saying, "I'm going into modelling when I leave Excelsis. Last year I took part in the student fashion show, and a scout from *Chandelle Elanga,* the London Fashion House, singled me out and invited me for a fashion shoot in London. I was there for a full day! They took pictures of me in hundreds of different outfits and different poses and complimented my looks and style. Would you like to see them?"

"Sure, when I can find a spare moment."

"They asked me to apply to them for a modelling job as soon as I finish my degree later this year." She felt sure she would be the one they picked from the nine other girls they had interviewed that day. As they ate their meal, she continued telling him about her London trip and the fashion artists she had met there. Russell was relieved when they headed to the dance floor because it brought a pause in her babbling about herself.

Couples were dancing in the Hall to the music of a local band called *Satin Seduction.* Russell and Goldie danced a couple numbers, but then others came to claim her, and she whirled away on the arm of a tall rugby type. Russell's irritation eased with her absence. Looking around, he was surprised to see Illovian. Although Zemki had lived in Benedict Hall a year or two before, he wasn't there now, so Russell assumed that a senior resident female must have invited him. He had seen Ambi, Sarah, Daniel, and Lawrence arrive together with Nthanda and Shuchun. They had taken the cheaper tickets for the entertainment only. Ambi and Nthanda had become friends after her visit to the church. Nthanda had found some fellow South Africans there that she could speak to in their own language which had helped to lessen her homesickness. She had thoroughly enjoyed the church experience and now attended most weeks.

Russell noticed Ambi was wearing a blue floral midi-shirred dress. As usual, she wasn't sporting any jewelry, and he couldn't detect any makeup. He thought the way her glossy hair framed her face gave her a look of glorious renaissance beauty. She danced with Daniel but then sat talking with Nthanda as Lawrence danced with Shuchun. Daniel danced several times with Sarah, and Russell observed the admiring looks she gave him. By now Goldie was fully occupied with a succession of partners. Russell thought he would explore the fairground attractions and the disco on offer in the marquees and adjoining rooms.

He exchanged smiles with Ambi on his way through to the nearest marquee. The first thing that caught his attention was a stand with a large portrait of Warden Victoria Sinclair. For a £1 donation, students were invited to guess her weight. The prize offered was a soft toy with Victoria's face cleverly stenciled on it. The proceeds would go to a local charity. Russell duly made his donation and signed his name and guess on a ticket that went into the mix. During the next hour or so he gave the fairground stalls a try. He had no luck at the coconut shy or at the hook-a-duck stand. The mini golf lawn in one corner looked inviting, and so he went round twice with varying success. About 2:00 a.m. he returned to learn who had won the weight-guessing prize. Nollum was ecstatic with delight when he heard his name announced. He hugged the toy warden, crooning, "ess, my precious!" and produced a ring from his pocket. It was too big for the toy's finger but fitted the wrist well. "My birthday present! my precious, we loves it!" he lisped, inserting the toy into his left breast pocket.

Just then Russell was startled to see the band leader, an African in appearance with spiky hair extensions, wearing a black, silver-studded velvet jacket and shiny leather jeans above white soled silver boots, cross the floor to speak to Ambi. He was even more amazed to see her get up, follow him to the stage, confer with the musicians, and then take the mike. The band struck up *World in Union,* the song often used to introduce the rugby football world cup event. Swiftly her soprano voice connected with the music, mounting with crystal clarity to fill the whole hall. As she sang about her dream of a world in harmony her wonderfully melodious voice galvanized attention. Students poured back into the hall to listen as her song spun a mood of hope and optimism. Electricity filled the air. When she reached the climactic notes of the song, soaring up toward the beginning of a new world destiny, a storm of applause burst out, particularly from the rugby club members. Shouts called for an encore. However, Ambi quickly handed the mike back to the band leader and slipped down to rejoin her friends.

Shaking himself to break the spell woven by the music, Russell found Goldie in the dance area with a group of admirers. She turned to him for a moment to tell him, "Ciao, I've been invited by these guys to go on to a night spot in Dunchester. I'm just leaving."

"OK, enjoy yourself!" He smiled his goodbye with a measure of relief. Turning round, he thought he detected an appealing look on Ambi's face and went over to where she was sitting with Nthanda and Shuchun. "Is there a problem?" he asked. With a look of relief, she said that Daniel had disappeared somewhere with Sarah. Nthanda and Shuchun were not used to late nights and alcohol. Would he help her escort them to their rooms? He readily agreed, and they guided the weary and slightly tipsy girls upstairs to their respective rooms. On the way back to the ballroom, he said, "Your rendering of *World in Union* was marvelous! Yours is an exceptionally lovely singing voice!"

Ambi smiled. "Thank you, I'm glad you enjoyed it. I love singing and couldn't resist the invitation here."

"How do you come to know the band leader. How did you learn to sing like that?"

"Oh, King Inanga is a member of my church. He leads the small orchestra that plays the music for our programs. That's how I learned to sing, from taking musical parts in the events the church puts on."

That surprised Russell. He'd thought church music was all dull routine hymns and psalms. "Does Daniel sing or play, too?"

"No, he's an accountant. He assists the church treasurer."

"Are you engaged to him?"

"My father would like me to marry him, but I'm not so sure we would suit each other. He has old-fashioned ideas about a wife's role."

"Would you like to try some of the fairground rides in the marquees?"

"Yes, I'm longing to get out there and see what's going on."

As they walked through to the marquees, Russell asked, "Why don't I ever see you drinking wine or beer?"

Ambi looked seriously at him before saying, "I believe a human being is made up of body, mind, and spirit with each component having a profound influence on the other. To keep in balance, you have to look after your physical wellbeing. Many studies have shown that the alcohol in even one drink is enough to impair motor and cognitive skills. I need all my brain cells functioning normally so I can stay in control of my thoughts, emotions, and behavior."

"Have you ever tried wine or spirits? A little alcohol helps to make events go more smoothly."

"Well, as far as I can, I avoid all alcoholic drinks, but occasionally so-called friends have played tricks on me by giving me beverages or food spiked with alcohol. Afterwards, I didn't enjoy the experience of getting tipsy and acting silly." As they entered the marquee, she inquired, "How is Melanie getting on?" Russell explained that he and Karl had persuaded her to go to the Fidem Health and Wellbeing Institute in a few days' time.

"That's wonderful. I'm sure it will make a big difference in her life. I've never actually been to the place, but I've heard Dr. Reade, one of the staff at Fidem, give excellent talks at our church on several occasions. He's quite a charismatic individual!"

Entering the marquee, they saw Nollum hugging his toy warden figure. Ambi giggled unselfconsciously at his antics. She was in whoops of laughter when they tried to play bar football. Although she got candy floss stuck to her face, it didn't bother her one bit. Russell had a go on the rodeo bull ride and managed to stay on board for almost the full time. Then she insisted on attempting it herself and laughed ruefully as she picked herself up after getting quickly tossed off. When Russell took a turn with her at the mini golf, he found that she was a quick learner. He realized she wasn't always serious but was fun to be with. The time passed rapidly as they tried almost everything offered. Finally, at about 4:00 a.m., Ambi announced with a yawn, "My eyelids are drooping. I'm about ready to crash. It's time to head off for some sleep."

Chapter 11. **A Puerile Prank**

THEY STROLLED BACK INTO the main hall and stopped for a final drink. While they were sitting at a table, Slab, Veronica, and their usual hangers-on joined them. Veronica sat next to Ambi, and Slab sat beside Russell. They seemed friendly for a change and complimented Ambi on her singing. The band was still playing, and couples were still dancing. Slab said *Satin Seduction* was a really cool band and, pointing to the leader, asked Ambi who he was, adding that she was lucky to know someone like him. However, Russell and Ambi were tired, so they finished their drinks quickly and stood up to leave. As they did, Russell felt strange. A feeling of weakness swept over him and his eyesight dimmed. The same happened to Ambi. Slab, Veronica, and their friends surrounded them and ushered them into the corridor outside the hall.

"It cost a lot, but that stuff we got from Zemki worked fast," Slab said. "I'm going into her," he added loudly.

"Absolutely and definitely not!" Veronica furiously retorted. "This is just a student prank. If you try to turn it into a criminal offence, we won't help, and we'll not stay silent. We stick to what we planned." Even Craig nodded agreement. He had warmed to Ambi's rugby song. Slab looked mutinous, but Veronica, Anna, and the rest hustled Ambi away to Veronica's room. Slab, Craig, and Nollum half marched, and half carried Russell along to Slab's room.

About two hours later, early on a chilly autumn day, Russell slowly regained consciousness. He had a terrible headache and was shivering. Slowly he tried to clear his head and take stock of what had happened. Finally, he realized that he was slumped on a wooden bench next to Ambi in what appeared to be a summer house. A car blanket had been thrown over the two of them. Russell was wearing only a pair of green shorts with a pattern of fig leaves. Next to him Ambi was clad in a green bikini with the same fig leaves pattern. Even in his groggy state he could see she had a near perfect figure with long graceful legs. Spotting a red apple on the floor nearby, his mind began to piece the situation together. They were in the Columburgh Botanic Garden and had been cast as Adam and Eve. No doubt someone had taken photos of Ambi offering him the apple, then they had been abandoned in the summer house.

Russell saw that his mobile phone had been left on the bench. After tucking the blanket round Ambi, he phoned Warden Victoria. Waking her up, he explained where they were, what he thought had happened, and asked her to bring overcoats for the both of them and two sample vials from the first-aid cabinet. As he was phoning, Ambi gradually regained consciousness, shivering violently. Her head ached and she felt confused and very frightened as she found herself with practically nothing on, next to a virtually naked and very muscular man. Clutching the blanket, she said shakily, "Where are we? Why have you brought me here?"

"I'm afraid we've both been victims of an unpleasant student prank. Our last drinks must have been spiked with a knock-out drug. I just re-gained consciousness myself a few moments ago, and I've phoned the War-den to come and get us." Ambi felt somewhat reassured by his calm manner and that he said the Warden was on her way.

"What is this all about do you think?"

Seeing her distress, he wanted to put a reassuring arm round her to keep her warm but knew that would only alarm her more. "Look around. We're in a garden and dressed in fig leaf costumes. We've been set up as Adam and Eve."

"Why would anyone do that?"

"Some people in that paleontology class object to your questioning Olympia, undermining her arguments. They figure we're ignorant and big-oted creationist Christians, and they're trying to teach us a lesson. My guess is that a photo of us in this garb will be circulated around the campus and on the internet to make us a laughingstock and damage our credibility." Russell kept talking calmly to try to reassure her. Although he looked care-fully around for any evidence, he could see nothing except trampled grass. Most likely the mobile phone had been wiped clean of fingerprints. Even the car blanket had no labels or markings.

The Botanic Garden was on the outskirts of Columburgh, only two or three miles from Benedict Hall, so the Warden reached them sooner than Russell had dared hope. She brought them warm overcoats, ushered them into her car, and drove them back to the Residence. There she took them straight to the infirmary and put a kettle on to boil for hot drinks while finding them dressing gowns.

"Have you any idea who did this and how it happened?" Victoria asked.

Ambi and Russell told her all they knew about the circumstances. A hot cup of tea began to clear Russell's head. He said he imagined it was a prank by students from the paleontology class who resented their questioning of evolution. "At the Ball we were both fine," he said, "until Roger, Veronica, and their group joined us for last drinks. They have often taken Ambi to task for the questions she asks and told her to lay off. Obviously, they must have planned this in advance and slipped something into our drinks. I expect they took photos of us as Adam and Eve and will use them to try to humiliate us and make us look foolish. I asked for the sample vials to collect a little of our blood to analyze for drugs. Do you think we should inform the police?"

"I wouldn't call the police," Victoria replied. "They're unlikely to investigate unless criminal damage or grievous bodily harm has been done. I'm going to ring for the nurse practitioner. It will be better if she collects the blood rather than you." Victoria knew from experience how easily such situations could escalate into nasty scandals. "I'm going to contact the University Principal and put her in the picture. I'll ask her to give the University IT services instructions to take down any such photos from all University networked devices. I'll also ask her to have a word with the local newspaper to request them not to publish. It's unlikely anything would reach them, but one never knows. Unfortunately, we won't be able to prevent students sharing photos on their personal devices. I'm also going to phone Ambi's father, explain what has happened, and suggest she goes home for a few days until this blows over."

The nurse practitioner arrived and withdrew small blood samples from them both. Russell insisted on the nurse giving him a small sample of his own blood and asked the Warden to let him know what the results were. He was very tired and took leave of them. After he had gone, Victoria said to Ambi, "I expect Slab and Veronica will deny everything and throw the blame on Russell. I know this is embarrassing but would you be willing to have a vaginal test?"

"I'm quite certain I wasn't raped."

"It's reassuring to hear that. But a DNA test would be a protection for your reputation and particularly for Russell's. Ugly rumors might well start circulating, and no amount of denials will quash them." Ambi saw the sense of what Victoria was suggesting, so she willingly provided samples to the nurse practitioner.

By now Benedict Hall had awakened. Victoria arranged for breakfast to be brought to Ambi in the sick room. Then she went to cleaning services and asked one of them to fetch day clothes for the girl from her room. Soon Mrs. Maggs appeared with a bundle of Ambi's clothes. "I came across these dumped outside your door, love," she said. "But this is your Ball dress, you'll need something else to go home in." Ambi was drooping from exhaustion but thanked her and asked her to get her jeans, a sweatshirt, and coat. Victoria told her to lie down for a while. Her father was coming to collect her soon.

Later, after Ambi had left with her father, another sub-warden rang Victoria and told her about a photograph of Ambi and Russell already circulating among the students. First, Victoria summoned Slab to her office. She questioned him about the Ball, where he had been, what time he had left, and who with. Then she asked him if he had anything to do with the photo of Ambi and Russell on social media. Flatly denying it, he declared, "I saw the two of them leaving together. I expect he switched her drink for alcohol. She wouldn't have any sort of head for that. It's not difficult to guess what he had in mind for her. I expect the photo is a souvenir he took, and someone hacked it out of his phone." Next Victoria summoned Veronica who told the same story, although less convincingly.

Chapter 12. **Toughing it Out**

RUSSELL HAD FOUND HIS clothes piled outside his room. He slept till after lunch, then showered and went out for some food. In the corridor Mrs. Maggs greeted him with, "I seen that photo of you and Ambi." The cleansing staff were always among the first to know any Hall gossip! "She looks dazed, poor dear. I know you wouldn't never do that to Miss Ambi. It's some nasty prank! I hope they nail the culprits and kick them out!"

"Thanks for your confidence! You're a brick!"

"It won't harm you that much dear. Most folk what sees it will be envious that both of you have such fine figures that you could model for swimsuit companies." Russell laughed at this, but she continued, "You ought to find yourself a nice girl to settle down with. You couldn't hardly do better than Ambi. She's a decent and hardworking person as well as bonny to look at."

Maybe she has a point at that, Russell thought as he went on his way.

During the next couple of days he buried himself in his routine of research along with lunchtime workouts at the gym. In the lab he caught an occasional knowing smirk on Zemki's face. The hostile looks he received from several of the residents of Benedict Hall bothered him a bit, but he ignored them. Ambi reappeared sooner than he expected. At breakfast, he asked her to join him for a drink in the Bishop's Arms that evening. They arrived almost at the same moment.

Over the lime juice he obtained for her, he asked, "How are you feeling? That was a grisly experience to go through."

"I'm OK. The break has reset me. I soon got the remnants of the drug out of my system, but the experience has made me feel rather insecure and distrustful of the other students. I look round wondering who could have planned that! Every time I pick up a drink, I taste it carefully in case it's spiked with something. Two or three students have called out 'Eve' after me, and one asked 'Will you be offering me an apple?' but it's all been good-humored joshing."

"How did your father react?"

"Warden Victoria told him the whole story as she knew it. She said she was fairly certain I hadn't been harmed in any way and that it was really intended just as a student prank. She mentioned I had been examined by the nurse practitioner and that she would let him know the results of the tests when they came in. In addition, she assured him that you had an unblemished record and that she had full confidence in you. Naturally, he was upset. He and my family fussed over me for a day or two, but I was missing vital lectures and other parts of my course, so I came back as soon as I felt reasonably at ease."

"It's good to see you again! I hope such a traumatic experience won't put you off my company forever! In a way it's made me feel a bit responsible for you!"

"Oh, no! It wasn't your fault in the least! You went through the same ordeal as I did."

"Have you seen the photo of us that's circulating?"

"Mrs. Maggs gave me a peek at it on her smart phone. It's very much like the temptation scene from Eden that you guessed it would be. We are mostly in profile so the doped expressions on our faces hardly show. They must have photoshopped out the arms of the students who were supporting us in those positions."

"I guess it could have been a lot worse. Actually, you looked great in that costume!" He told her what Mrs. Maggs had said the student reaction would be, and a shy smile crossed Ambi's face.

"I would never take up modelling! What a boring job! What a self-regarding waste of a life!"

"I agree with you! Seems a shallow empty kind of life to me, too." The contrast between Ambi's and Goldie's views of modelling suddenly struck him. He noticed how unpretentious Ambi was and her lack of pride about her appearance. "Will you be able to make up for the lectures you lost?"

"It shouldn't be a problem. Nthanda and Shuchun attend my classes, and they already offered to lend me their lecture notes."

"It's good when you have a family to rally round and support you through tough times."

"You're right. My father, mother, and little sister Rosalinda live nearby in Dunchester, and they all helped me. My elder brother David is grown up and on his own. Of course, we have grandparents, uncles, and aunts, but they don't live near here."

"I'll be interested to hear the results of the tests, but I'm afraid we'll never be able to pin the blame for sure on Slab and Veronica. I'm just going to tough it out the next few days. There's so much going on in the months before Christmas that it will soon be forgotten." They walked back to Benedict together in time for dinner, admiring the autumn colors on the way.

A day or two later Warden Victoria texted Ambi and Russell with the results of the tests. Ambi's test showed nothing but her own DNA. The blood analyses disclosed a drug of the benzodiazepine class in both their samples. The test notes reported it was a relative of Rohypnol but wasn't in the library of drugs accessible to the laboratory. Probably it was a new variety of date-rape drug.

Russell had access in his laboratory to powerful analytical spectrometers. He had retained a sample of his own blood, so he extracted it with solvent, filtered it, and set about analyzing the contents. Soon he found that its structure was indeed the same as the one he had seen weeks ago in Zemki's laboratory notebook. He recognized it as a key bit of evidence, but on its own it would not be enough to pin anything on either Illovian or Slab.

Warden Victoria suspected that the stories Slab and Veronica were telling had started ugly rumors about Russell circulating. She called a meeting in her office of all the Benedict security, catering, and cleansing staff, plus all the sub-wardens except Russell. "You all know of the unpleasant prank played on two of our students recently," she began. "I think that ugly rumors are smearing Russell's character." Mrs. Maggs and several others confirmed this. "I've had the results of DNA tests on Ambi and blood tests for both her and Russell," the Warden continued. "No DNA except her own was found on Ambi—she wasn't raped. Furthermore, a date-rape drug related to Rohypnol was detected in the blood samples from both of them," then she repeated, "From both of them! That indicates Russell was drugged and just as much an innocent victim as was Ambi. I'd like you all to spread the truth about the circumstances as widely as possible. Vigorously confront anyone who casts aspersions on Russell. Are there any questions?"

Hands were raised, and she was asked, "Have you any idea who was really behind it?"

"We have a fair idea of who did it, but there's no proof. If we name them, we, and the University, could lay ourselves open to libel charges. The testing laboratory reported that this is a new and more potent date-rape drug. It may be used again. I want all of you to be alert for any suspicious activities. Keep your eyes open. We want all our students to be completely safe. I'm going to pin up a notice informing students that someone is selling this drug, warning them to be on the alert, and asking them to report to me any information they may have."

Mrs. Maggs reported to Russell about the meeting with the Warden. Knowing how the Hall staff were adept at spreading gossip, he considered it a wise move on Victoria Sinclair's part. He also noticed a distinct lessening in hostility toward him during the next few days. Two students even approached him to tell him they had heard the whole story and had "never really doubted" him!

His research was progressing well. The Friday for him to start working at MoliMart arrived. When he checked in with security at their main gate, someone escorted him up to Dr. Irma Vonvoigt's office. Cautiously welcoming him to the Innovative Research Team, she repeated much of what he had heard before about MoliMart's beneficent aims to improve the health and wellbeing of society. Then she took him to the secretariat, where he received a white coat and a list of protocols about health and security. He signed for an ID and key card that gave him access to parts of the complex. Next, she introduced him to IT services where he chose a password and username enabling him to access MoliMart's network. He wasn't allowed to network his own laptop but was assigned a MoliMart computer already loaded with an e-lab book, digitally connected to a central server. Access to it was restricted to senior research personnel and management and it was administered by MoliMart's IT services. All his experiments, notes, and reports would be recorded that way. Finally, they handed him the key to a company car which turned out to be a small and, he thought, boring Dacia Sandero. Finally, he had to sign a lengthy document outlining his responsibilities as its temporary custodian and absolving MoliMart from any blame in connection with his use of it.

Back in her office, Dr. Irma asked him to brief her on the current state of his research. Expecting it, he had come prepared. On his laptop he opened a PowerPoint and took her through all the information he thought she was entitled to know about his *longiferase* work. She asked questions and made criticisms in her officious way that he answered guardedly. Stating that the project was important to MoliMart, she assured him that the company would provide all necessary resources. Then she took him to the lab where he would be working and introduced Norman Odham, the technical officer there. Odham quickly closed whatever he had been watching on his computer and flashed a look of deferential delight to Dr. Irma. "Show Russell his workbench and the desk he can use in the open plan office," she directed. "Then give him the usual tour of the complex."

"Sure thing, Dr. Irma," he said in way that Russell felt was somewhat obsequious.

Norman took his time showing Russell round all the biochemical research and administrative parts of the complex. One area in the original country mansion part was strictly private and off limits. "Your ID card won't open the metal doors there," he explained. "Nobody really knows what goes on there, but strange sounds can sometimes be heard." Russell already had a fair idea of the layout of the whole complex from the time his father's company had a contract to extend and remodel it. He guessed the restricted area housed facilities for animal testing of new MoliMart products. In a whisper Norman warned Russell to stay clear of the security officers. "Little Hitler's they are. Watch out for the dogs they release at night—they're real brutes."

While coffee and tea were available from machines and there was a small on-site café, Russell had bought his own snack lunch. He spent the afternoon familiarizing himself with the protein synthesizing equipment, centrifuges, ultrasonic disintegrators, and gel electrophoresis apparatus as well as the protocols for using the e-lab book. Then he picked up his car, a second-hand model, from the MoliMart car depository and drove back to Benedict Hall. While he had driven his father's car many times, he still felt a small thrill to be in charge of this one, even though it was only a small dull model on loan. It would be adequate to give him the freedom of the road.

Chapter 13. **Olympia as Scientist and Socialite**

THE NEXT WEDNESDAY, RUSSELL took his seat in Olympia's paleontology lecture with a keen sense of anticipation. Would Ambi's drugging experience have cowed her into staying quiet? Olympia was holding forth about *cetaceans*, commonly known as whales. Her PowerPoint contained beautiful reconstructions of complete skeletons taken from displays at the University of Michigan Museum of Paleontology, the Natural History Museum in London, and the Smithsonian Institution in Washington, D.C. They included true whales from the *Basilosaurids* to modern ones. She described the classification of whales with the two additional types, the *Mysticeti* (baleen whales) and the *Odontoceti* (toothed whales).

Toward the end of her talk, she moved on to fossil evidence for whale evolution. "About 50 million years ago one species of land mammal went back into the water and evolved into whales. The whale fossils provide one of the grandest and most complete demonstrations of animal evolution. We have fossils all the way from land dwelling quadrupeds, through intermediate 'walking whales,' right through to the *Basilosaurids*," she declared.

She backed up her statement by showing reconstructions of the skeletons and artists' impressions of three intermediate "walking whales," *Pakicetus*, *Ambulocetus*, and *Rhodocetus*. Olympia told them that the skulls of the three intermediate creatures contained features typical of whales, including blow holes and ear bones with finger-like projections known as "sigmoid processes," also typical of whales. The artists' reconstructions depicted feet intermediate between hoofs and flippers. "All the evidence of the evolutionary transition is there," she proclaimed. "This is a triumph of evolutionary theory confirmed by field evidence!"

At this point Russell was fascinated to see Ambi's hand go up for a question. Half-suppressed groans erupted from the group around Slab and Veronica. Olympia looked impatient but nodded for Ambi to go ahead.

"The pictures you showed were reconstructions of *Pakicetus's* skull and skeleton made from just a few fossil bone fragments," she began. "When more complete fossils were found, it was discovered that *Pakicetus* had no blow hole or sigmoid process. The fossilized feet bones found later indicated the creature was purely a land animal. The *Ambulocetus* story was similar. Those depiction you have been presenting are misleading. The fossil feature claimed to be a sigmoid process was nothing like that of a whale, and a number of experts dismissed the supposed whale characteristics as illusory. As for *Rhodocetus,* the flippers and whale-like fluke were just added by the artist—no corresponding fossil bones have been found. It's disingenuous of museums to keep displaying such pictures when the evidence to support them is really lacking."

Olympia looked thunderous as she retorted, "The evidence I've shared represents the considered opinion of the top experts in paleontology and evolutionary biology. The most prestigious institutes in the world back it up! This is consensus science of the first order. Only peripheral mavericks and individuals biased by religious bigotry dispute it." She wound up her lecture, distributed worksheets, and stalked out, looking irritated.

Russell, Nthanda, Shuchun, and Lawrence clustered round Ambi to lend her support as the students streamed out of the lecture hall. Even Craig seemed impressed with Ambi's apparent background knowledge of the subject. Seeing the group around her, Slab, Veronica, and his cronies left the area with sullen expressions.

"Is that true about the imaginary character of those whale fossil reconstructions?" Craig asked Ambi.

"It absolutely is, and I can send you references to the scientific literature backing my statements if you're interested."

An outdoors type who had little time for reading science articles, Craig said hastily, "No need to do that! You do realize you're starting to get Olympia seriously annoyed? She's not one to take that lying down and will find a way of making you suffer!"

"I can't help that. Following the evidence wherever it leads should be an absolute moral imperative for us all. Whatever the consequences. The way human and animal life came into existence has enormous significance. It's absolutely basic to both religion and philosophy. Getting a right understanding about it must be one of the most important things we do in life."

By now Russell and Ambi had fallen into the habit of meeting regularly for a drink at the Bishop's Arms during the evenings after Olympia's lectures. Her courage to keep up her questioning impressed him. It recalled to his mind the Chinese proverb, "He who asks a question is a fool for five minutes. He who remains silent is a fool forever." Would he have the same moral fortitude when faced with moral dilemmas?

One Wednesday Ambi told him that the CC Club had blackballed her and her application for membership was unsuccessful. "I'm disappointed," she said. "I would have liked the experience of helping in their charitable enterprises as well as having a lifetime support group." Feeling that it would only add insult to injury, Russell didn't tell her about the hostile message that had accompanied her application. So, he just sympathized and said how unfair he thought it was. Ambi also told him she was worried about the poor grades she was getting on her written submissions for the paleontology course. "I get top grades for all my other geoscience courses," she explained. "It's not that my answers are wrong, but Olympia writes comments like 'trite' or 'poorly reasoned' or 'disjointed' on my work."

"I hope she hasn't taken a dislike to you," he remarked. "It would be a good idea to have a word with your Adviser of Studies. Explain that you get top grades in all your other courses and can't understand why they are so bad in paleontology." When Ambi followed his advice, her Adviser later told her that Olympia stoutly defended her marking, saying that Ambi was out of date and confused and needed to get her head round modern developments.

Early in December, Olympia invited the whole paleontology class to her place on Wednesday evening for mince pies and drinks. Anticipation spread among the students at the prospect of a social get together with her. She was married to Alastair Sheldrake-Smith, the CEO of the multinational asset management company, Endgame Capital. He owned property in London and New York, but they lived much of their time in a mansion near Columburgh.

Russell had offered lifts in his car, to Ambi, Nthanda, and Lawrence. Ambi wore her pale blue dress. She'd arranged her hair in waves that descended from a circular braid to her shoulders. Nthanda had on her traditional South African outfit of a multicolor beaded tribal top and beaded mini apron above a white skirt. Russell and Lawrence had both chosen dark jackets with clean blue jeans. "You both look awesome today," Russell told Ambi. "We're lucky to be seen with you!"

"Oh, boy! You're a stylish pair," Lawrence chipped in.

As they drove along, they all speculated animatedly about what they could expect that evening at Olympia's place. Several majestic English Oak trees graced the lawns flanking the driveway to the mansion. Russell noticed one particularly magnificent specimen towering above the others with wide spreading branches. In the twilight, the ground underneath appeared as a golden litter of fallen leaves and acorns. They entered the Georgian mansion through its twin-columned portico, joining the throng of students being greeted by Olympia and Alastair. Referring to a list, Olympia named them one by one to her husband. He gave Ambi a questioning look as in a jocular tone, Olympia called her, "My special bête noir." The girls followed a sign saying "Ladies Cloakroom" to a room on the right. Russell and Lawrence were directed across the marble flagged hallway into the spacious great hall decorated with a huge Christmas tree covered in colored lights, tinsel, candy canes, and small wrapped parcels. A large flashing star topped it. A Santa, riding in a toy-laden sleigh drawn by Disney-style reindeer covered one wall. Strings of LED lights, candles, and garlands of holly heightened the Christmas mood. A large spray of mistletoe hung above the main exit.

A central table held dishes of hot mince pies and a selection of drinks together with piles of Christmas crackers. Russell and Lawrence collected paper plates and joined the throng of students helping themselves. Noise from the animated conversations occurring all around the room drowned out the Christmas music playing in the background. Russell circulated among the group, exchanging Christmas greetings particularly with "his" students from Benedict Hall. To his surprise, Alastair accompanied Olympia into the room. He'd thought the magnate would have retired to his own sanctum after greeting everyone. Tall with graying hair and a military style moustache, he wore an expression of tolerant good humor, but his gray eyes were watchful and intelligent. He seemed a jovial type and was making students laugh as he drifted from one to another. Slab made a beeline for Olympia and was dropping what, from her appreciative expression, looked like compliments into her ear. Russell reckoned he was trying to maneuver her under the mistletoe.

Veronica was not pleased, however. Coming over to flirt with Russell, she asked, "Not doing an Adam impersonation this evening?"

"Only at garden parties," he replied, looking amused. Just then Alastair joined them and asked, "How do trees access the internet?" As they both looked blank, he said, "They log on." Russell laughed and decided to save that one for Mrs. Maggs. Alastair asked Veronica what she planned to do for Christmas and learned that she was expecting to go home for a large family party, but also hoped to do a show in London. Looking at them both, he asked, "Did you notice our oak trees as you were arriving? We're very proud of them. They're splendidly beautiful specimens that were planted hundreds of years ago, and they're part of our contribution toward conserving the environment."

"One especially grand and imposing specimen stood out and was taller than the others," Russell commented. Looking gratified, Alastair asked Russell for his name. "That one's Olympia's special favorite tree," he said. "She's been known to hug it, calls it her Tree of Life, and has named it 'Beagle' after the oaken ship Darwin made his explorations in. What are your plans when you finish Olympia's paleontology course?"

"Paleontology is just a side-line for me. I'm doing postgraduate research into longevity with Sir George Faircross, sponsored by MoliMart."

That got Alastair's full attention. "Are you making any progress?"

"Yes. We're investigating a new method of elongating the end proteins of chromosomes. Studies with bugs have provided promising results. I'm particularly working with software visualization and prediction tools."

"You must tell me more about this some time. But I would be wary of MoliMart, my boy. I've nothing specific against them, but there are rumors they have overextended themselves. They've been involved in dubious deals on the money market with companies suspected of money laundering and with some very shady Middle Eastern organizations." Startled, Russell's expression showed his concern. "Don't invest in their shares and don't plan on a long-term future with them," Alastair concluded.

Russell knew it could be valuable advice from a financial expert such as Sheldrake-Smith. "What do you advise I invest in?" he asked curiously.

"That's a burning question! One I lose sleep over. If you want a serious answer, you'll need to take out an account with Endgame Capital. But it's no secret we've been buying into AlternoPharm." With that he moved on, and Veronica said, "I think you made a good impression there! What are you doing for Christmas?" Before Russell could answer, Slab joined them. He'd consumed a lot of alcohol, and glaring at Russell, said, "You stay away from Veronica, and that goes for Ambi too. They're my preserve."

68

"Don't be ridiculous, you're not an oriental potentate with a harem or a pop idol besieged by groupies!" Veronica hissed as she dragged Slab away. Russell had a fair idea a showdown was looming between himself and Slab, and he expected it would be a physical one. Glancing around, he saw several pairs of students laughingly taking advantage of the mistletoe.

Nthanda's colorful outfit had attracted a lot of interest. An admiring group had gathered round her and Ambi, as she told them about the African traditions behind the patterns and the bead work. "Unmarried women wear this set of beads," she said, pointing to her beaded apron. "Married women have completely different outfits."

"Can girls from your culture choose any man they like?" Ambi asked.

"It's not as simple as that. Usually, an uncle will act as a marriage broker. Bride prices are the norm in my area, and he will negotiate with suitors."

"How much does a bride cost?"

"Up to six cows are usually given. In a way it's an insurance that the suitor is a responsible person. He'll have to borrow from his relatives and friends to raise the price. The fact that they trust him enough to lend, shows he's serious and dependable."

A voice from the back of the cluster of students called out, "I'll give seven cows for you!"

Nthanda peered round but couldn't make out who it was. "Sounds a good offer," she said with a twinkle. "But you'll have to speak to my uncle, I'll give you his email address."

Soon all the mince pies had disappeared, and Alastair began tapping his glass for attention. As the room quietened, he announced, "Attention everyone! Take your glasses because my wife has a toast to propose." Looking regal and raising her glass, Olympia intoned, "May you never forget what is worth remembering or remember what is best forgotten! Specially at the exams! Happy Christmas everyone!" Raising their glasses, they all echoed, "Happy Christmas."

"Everyone may take something from the Christmas tree," she added. Many of the students correctly interpreted it as a signal that it was time to be leaving. Russell sought out Olympia and thanked her and Alastair for a lovely party. He said he hoped they would have a wonderful Christmas. "We'll all be ready for more paleontology in the New Year, and we're specially looking forward to the field trip."

"I'm arranging a special place for our fossil field trip in the spring," she said. "You won't be disappointed."

Russell rounded up Lawrence, Ambi, and Nthanda, and they headed back to Benedict Hall in his car, talking animatedly. "What did you get from the tree?" Russell asked them.

"I got a party blower," Ambi said, unrolling it toward his face. He made the car swerve, and the girls shrieked. "I got a chocolate Santa," Nthanda announced.

Lawrence showed the toy Rudolf he had bagged. "Its nose lights when you pull its tail."

Ambi told them Alastair had come up to her and asked why his wife had called her a bête noir. "I told him, 'Because I ask a lot of questions in her lectures.'" He said, 'That should be a good thing. Universities are supposed to be where students can ask questions.'

"'Yes,' I replied, 'but my questions challenge her cherished theory of evolution.'"

"'Oh, she won't like that,' he replied. 'Evolution is meat and drink to her. She wouldn't take kindly to her creed being questioned.'"

"'You speak as if you might not share her views,' I observed."

"'Well, I'm essentially a businessman dealing with verifiable facts,' he answered."

"Then he moved on," Ambi concluded, "saying that 'What happened in the far past couldn't really be known, and it was better to keep an open mind.'"

"He's a really shrewd character," Russell remarked. "I was surprised he stayed for the party, but I now think he was there looking to pick up ideas and to see if Olympia's class had any really promising students."

As Russell was parking, Ambi mentioned the Carol Service coming up in the University Chapel in a week's time. "Why don't you all come along," she said. "The Excelsis Vocal Ensemble will be singing. It'll be a very special experience." Nthanda was enthusiastic, and Russell and Lawrence both said they would think it over.

Chapter 14. **Transforming Times**

RUSSELL WAS NOT ENJOYING his workdays at MoliMart. He thought Dr. Irma a hopeless supervisor. She crept up quietly behind him at all hours, checking on what he was doing. Unfortunately, she offered no intellectual input to the project whatsoever nor was she any help in interpreting any of the readings from the spectrometers or other instruments. Her style was that of a bureaucratic manager, constantly urging him to meet unrealistic targets she had set herself. As she read through his e-lab reports she would add commas and make other minor amendments that she labeled as "mistakes." She even snooped around for drawers he had left open, apparatus that needed cleaning, and small spillages that required wiping up. Then she added them to the count she kept of his alleged "mistakes." Each day, she would flaunt in front of Russell a graph she was keeping of the number of such "mistakes" relative to the days he had been working and insisted that he keep it moving downward. He avoided her as much as he possibly could.

Zemki had started working alongside him at MoliMart. Russell noticed he had no trouble with Dr. Irma. Even worse, Zemki followed the same fawning as Norman Odham. He greeted her effusively. Complimented her appearance. Said "Yes, Dr.," and "No, Dr." to her every utterance. Brought her coffee from the machine. Once Russell heard him asking her to meet him for a drink in a local Pub. It was a relief to return to Benedict in the evenings, and he was thankful Christmas was approaching when he would get a break from her hassle.

Most days, on his way from Benedict Hall to the lab, Russell passed St. Margaret's Chapel in the heart of Excelsis University. The rare and beautiful gothic building had survived the upheaval of the Reformation. The outside presented a succession of masonry bays, each containing a stained-glass window between the substantial buttresses. A high clock and bell tower adjoined the west end. On the inside at the east end, a stone communion table and the surrounding sanctuary were decorated with glorious mosaics depicting scenes from the Bible. A high ceiling of dark wood paneling, with flower-like details picked out in gold leaf, surmounted the stained-glass windows and the richly carved wooden choir stalls. The west end, beneath the tower, contained a balcony housing a magnificent modern pipe organ and more stalls for the choir. On days when sunshine poured through the stained-glass windows, visitors would comment on its beauty and marvel at its atmosphere evocative of ancient piety and serenity. Russell himself had never been to a service there or even looked inside. But he determined he would go to the carol service on Wednesday.

Dressing warmly on a cold December evening, he accepted the service sheet, found a seat in the stalls, and watched as the chapel filled to over-flowing. Ambi, Nthanda, and Shuchun took seats on the opposite side. As a lifetime atheist he was uneasy about what was in store, but he relaxed as the organ played contemplative introductory music. The service proceeded as a series of readings from the Bible about the birth of Jesus Christ. The different accents and expressions of the students and staff chosen to present them intrigued him—some pious, some sincere, and some nervous. Carols and songs sung by the choir and audience interspersed the readings. The stone walls and high ceiling added a special resonance to the music. To his surprise, he felt himself somehow transported to a higher plane as the choir sang, in parts, their first carol, "The Angel Gabriel from Heaven Came," and later "Sing Lullaby." He felt the force of centuries of passionate upward yearn-ing carrying him along. Although he felt a little uncomfortable during the prayers, the melodies more than compensated. On his way out he privately acknowledged that the service had had a profound effect on him. *Could it be true that God had come down to earth as a baby?* He mused.

After dipping into the books Ambi had recommended, he couldn't in all honesty deny that Jesus Christ was a real person who had lived and died more or less as tradition told. But the idea of a God-man was very counter intuitive, he felt. Then it passed through his mind that lots of things in na-ture were counter intuitive. A being extraordinary enough to be the creator of the universe might well be expected to do counter-intuitive things.

By the end of the week Benedict Hall would close to the undergradu-ates for the Christmas and New Year break. It wouldn't reopen till the start of the new semester later in January. At breakfast on Friday, Russell joined Ambi, Nthanda, Shuchun, and Lawrence and asked them what their plans were for the holidays. Nthanda and Shuchun both had relatives living near London and were going to join them. Lawrence said he was flying home to New England. Ambi would head to a family Christmas at her home in Dunchester. She asked Russell if he would see Melanie during the holidays, and he told her she would be returning from the Health Spa in a few days. "Why don't you bring her to my church?" Ambi suggested. "We have a Christmas service open to the public. The lively music eases anxieties. It could do her a lot of good."

"Thanks for the suggestion. I'll see what she has to say."

Russell had bought a book of jokes and a box of Dairy Milk chocolates for Mrs. Maggs. Later that day he sought her out. "Happy Christmas! Thanks a million for keeping my room spotless. Here's a clutch of clean jokes for a cleaning lady."

Smiling her thanks, she asked, "What did the stamp say to the Christmas card?"

"Fancy a close encounter?"

"No! Stick with me, and we'll go places!"

Laughing, he inquired, "Will you be seeing Arthur over Christmas?"

"Yes, and I'll be sharing these chocolates with him."

Russell wished her a wonderful time, then sought out Warden Victoria. He thanked her warmly for all her help and bade her goodbye till the New Year.

A text message from his father had arrived telling him that Melanie would be returning from the Fidem Health Spa that weekend, and that he should come home to help welcome her if he could manage it. Collecting a few things, he headed home that evening. The next day he took turns with Karl driving to Wales in his father's Range Rover to pick her up.

As soon as they set eyes on her, it was obvious that a momentous change had taken place. It was a Melanie they hadn't seen for years. Neatly dressed, her hair styled, her eyes sparkling, she seemed full of energy as she literally ran over to them. She could hardly wait till she was in the car to start enthusiastically recounting her time at Fidem.

Once registered, she had been shown to a nicely furnished room with a view of the hills. A group of five guests had started courses that weekend. They had all met over a light evening meal. Dr. Regius Reade had introduced himself before handing each of them a descriptive course booklet and a booking card. He asked them to look over all the activities and decide which ones they intended to take part in. In addition, he strongly urged them to attend his talks on holistic physical, mental, and spiritual health. "We'll meet again over breakfast tomorrow and finalize plans."

Melanie admitted she had initially felt indifferent to everything. All the guests were advised to give up alcohol completely, and she had struggled with this for the first few days. But now she was enthusiastic about the whole program. The regular fitness exercise classes to rhythmic music had released endorphins in her brain and strengthened her muscles. The daily swimming and sauna had cleansed her system of toxins, real and imagined. The fresh air, sunshine, and natural beauty of the countryside walks in the hills had refreshed and recharged her jaded mind. She'd thrived on the lentil and bean soups, the vegetarian lasagna, the vegetarian cassoulet, the chickpea vegetarian curry, the celeriac and tahini potato gratin and the risotto with radishes and cherry tomatoes, all accompanied by a profusion of fresh fruit salads.

Dr. Regius's daily presentations had made the biggest impression on her. A tall, dark-haired, charismatic individual approaching middle-age, he had a sympathetic but firm manner. His clear blue eyes seemed to see into everything but with a wise rather than a prying manner. He used PowerPoints and video clips to show how amazingly unique and exceptional human life was. Melanie had loved his demonstrations of how incredibly special the properties of water, oxygen, carbon dioxide, and sunlight were. How they were tailored to suit life by allowing sunlight of just the right wavelength through the atmosphere. He demonstrated a host of ways in which the environment was specially designed to support not just life but particularly human life.

In one of his talks describing the discovery of the fine tuning of the universe's physical parameters, Dr. Regius had shown stunning photographs of star clusters and galaxies. His description of the incredibly fine balance of the gravitational and nuclear forces keeping giant stars and miniscule atoms in place, opened her eyes to see they must have been put in place by a cosmic Designer. Affirming that such a Designer could only be God, he offered graphic examples showing the close interconnection of human physical, mental, and spiritual health. The spiritual dimension had not been previously part of Melanie's worldview. Dr. Regius offered numerous examples of lives that had changed from hopeless depression to vitality as they had embraced spiritual renewal and faith in God.

Finally, Melanie told Russell and Karl of how he had presented compelling evidence from history, from archaeology, and from the remarkable fulfilment of specific prophecies, that the Bible was completely trustworthy and an authentic spiritual guide. As he listened to her enthusiastic recital, Russell remembered the books Ambi had recommended to him, and determined to read them carefully during the holiday. Although their father was skeptical, he was so relieved to see such a transformed Melanie that he kept his mouth shut.

The change in Melanie persisted as she resumed her job in Karl's business, putting his office accounting records in order. Then finding an online course in business management, she registered and began it. In addition, she located a nearby gym and regularly attended fitness classes. She told her brother that Dr. Regius belonged to the Fidem Adventus Christi Church in Dunchester. They were advertising a Christmas service on Saturday, and she asked Russell to accompany her there.

Chapter 15. **Christmas Excursion**

RUSSELL'S ATHEIST BELIEFS HAD been taking a battering from its dire effects in Melanie's life and his betrayal by the confirmed atheist Sir George Faircross. The unforgiveable behavior inflicted on Ambi especially disturbed him. Why did those who claimed to defend evolution and naturalism think it necessary to insult and intimidate her? Could it be an unconscious sense that the concepts were somehow failures? Olympia's inadequate responses to Ambi's comments during the paleontology lectures had raised questions about evolution in his mind. In addition, he'd been avoiding the Sceptics Society meetings for several weeks. As for now, he had no idea what to expect from attending church and was a little afraid that Melanie had been brainwashed. However, she showed none of the fanatical or closed-mind behavior he would have expected in that case. Partly out of brotherly affection and partly out of curiosity, he agreed to go with her. It dismayed Karl to learn that both his children were planning to attend a religious service. Still, he didn't say much, because he was so pleased that Melanie had not only left alcoholism behind but had apparently regained her mental balance. Furthermore, he expected that what they would witness at the church would only disgust them.

Christmas Day dawned cold and crisp but dry. Karl had booked them a traditional Christmas dinner at the Dunchester Castle Restaurant. They arranged to meet him there after the church service. Before Melanie and Russell left to find the Fidem Adventus Christi Church, their father warned them not to let themselves be taken in by any clever Christian propaganda or financial ploys.

The church was a modern building situated in a modest suburb. They parked the car and joined the people streaming toward the main entrance.

A wide pillared doorway led to a spacious, white painted foyer, off which the main auditorium and several ancillary rooms branched.

A large African woman dressed in a colorful national costume greeted them at the door. At first, she seemed rather imposing until her wide smile revealed perfect white teeth that lit up her face. She welcomed Melanie and Russell warmly, gave them a printed program, and invited them to sit anywhere they liked. More people shook their hands as they entered the main sanctuary. It had chairs with padded seats arranged in three banks facing a wide platform. Melanie and Russell found seats and looked around with interest. Flower arrangements brightened the platform and the walls of the sanctuary. A large Christmas tree, decorated with tinsel, miniature candles, and small wrapped parcels, stood to one side. A nativity scene, complete with an infant in a manger, occupied the opposite wall. Two huge LCD monitors, high up on each side of the platform, flashed a welcoming message. A small orchestra began assembling in front, while a pianist quietly played Christmas themed hymns. A choir was gathering on the platform.

By 11:00 a.m., the auditorium had filled almost to capacity. The orchestra started playing a Christmas introit based on "Joy to the World." Looking closely at the pianist, Russell began to wonder if he could be King Inanga, the leader of the band at the Benedict Hall Ball. He was dressed completely differently in a sober dark suit, but his presence aroused Russell's curiosity. As he turned his attention to the choir, a pleasant jolt coursed through him as he recognized Ambi in the center of the front row. This must be her church, the one she had invited him to! Nudging Melanie, he whispered, "There's Ambi in the choir." But Melanie didn't respond, because the only time she had met Ambi she had been too drunk to remember.

Russell had half expected the service to consist of solemn processions of vestment-clad clergy, incense, and bell ringing. Alternatively, judging by the religious channels he had occasionally seen on TV, he guessed a charismatic individual would take the stage, holding a Bible and ranting about hell and damnation on one hand or the possibility of wonderful prosperity on the other, interspersed with appeals for money. To his pleasant surprise, a dignified woman began the service with a simple opening prayer, followed by popular carols sung by the choir. Readings and poems about the birth of Christ interspersed the music. The words of the carols appeared on the monitor screens.

After the announcement of a "Children's Time" with Mrs. Amhurst, all the girls and boys in the audience gathered to sit at the front, facing the audience. She asked them if they knew the story of Jesus' birth and if they were good at making faces. Most nodded, though some looked doubtful. She then invited the children to imitate the expressions of the individuals in the Christmas story. First, they were to copy the anxious face of Joseph as he guided Mary to Bethlehem. The children eagerly presented furrowed brows and fingers to teeth. Then Mrs. Amhurst called for the innkeeper's face as he refused them a room. The children shook heads, pursed lips, and waved them away with their hands. Next, she asked for Mary's happy face when baby Jesus was born. All produced wide smiles and crinkled eyes. Laughter came from the adults as one boy gave a thumbs-up. To demonstrate the shepherd's fright when the angels appeared, the children displayed open mouths and wide eyes. The wise men's reverence was more challenging, but two or three managed to look upwards with hands clasped in prayer. When questioned what expressions Joseph and Mary would have shown when the Magi gave Jesus gold, frankincense, and myrrh, some said happiness, others excitement, and a few gratitude. Finally, she suggested Herod's angry face. All the children were good at screwing up their eyes, baring their teeth and shaking their fists.

"What face should you have shown your parents when you opened your Christmas presents?" Mrs. Amhurst inquired. Two children instantly announced "gratitude." "It's always right to say, 'thank you,'" she told them. "And if you forgot, there's still time to make up for it." The kids skipped back to their places still practicing making faces.

Ambi sang, "O Come, O Come, Emmanuel," backed by the orchestra and with the choir softly echoing, "rejoice, rejoice," at intervals. The haunting music filled the auditorium, as her velvet voice proclaimed, "Rejoice! Rejoice! Emmanuel, shall come to thee, O Israel." The heart-warming harmonies would echo in Russell's mind for hours afterward.

What Russell guessed was a group of youth from the church put on a short Christmas skit parodying the "no room at the inn" story in a modern hotel setting. A harassed landlord exchanged witty comments with his assistant as he turned away a squad of drunken Roman soldiers, three rich princelings from the Middle East, and finally directed a heavily pregnant Mary and Joseph to a nearby cattle shed.

The preacher for the main service was a distinguished-looking man in his late 40s, wearing a business suit with a colorful geometric patterned tie. His dark brown hair was tinged with gray, he had a well-trimmed beard and moustache, and wore gold-framed glasses. He spoke with a resonant voice in tones of persuasive reasonableness. A succession of PowerPoint graphics illustrated his short sermon on the LCD screens. He began with a remarkable, but true, story of how a woman in Michigan, USA, had posted a Christmas present to her daughter in Prestwick, Scotland, during the Second World War. The ship carrying it had been torpedoed with great loss of life. Amazingly, her parcel had floated all the way to a beach near Prestwick. A beachcomber had found it with the address still legible, so miraculously, it had been delivered to her daughter only two days after Christmas!

He then spoke of God's remarkable gift to humankind. That the eternal, Creator God, took on Himself human nature and was born to the Virgin Mary. That the infinite God of perfect goodness was willing to be born as a baby and subject Himself to material human nature was a remarkable demonstration of His love for humanity and the unlimited value He placed on human life. The pastor concluded by urging the audience to follow the divine example of generosity and kindness, not only by giving gifts at Christmas but also throughout the year. The service ended with everyone singing the carol, "Joy to the World," followed by a short benediction.

Russell had expected to be either bored or repelled, but the service had kept his attention throughout. He had enjoyed the music and been fascinated by the other items. The only call for money had been a low-key retiring offering, and he gave generously to that. As he and Melanie were leaving, a friendly woman approached and invited them to come to the adjacent hall for mince pies and a hot drink. Ambi and Daniel appeared, greeted them warmly, and repeated the invitation. Melanie explained that they already had a lunch engagement that prevented them from accepting. They both smilingly thanked Ambi and praised her singing. "The choir and orchestra are the ones to thank," she modestly replied. "What did you make of the sermon? You know it was my father who preached it?"

Russell's eyes widened. "Short and sweet, goes down a treat," he said. "I'm starting to doubt that all sermons are boring. Pastor's kids are supposed to be rebels, but you don't seem to conform?"

"That's because my father isn't a typical pastor. He's not a hypocrite, he's not boring, and he gives good reasons for what he believes."

"Our father is just about the opposite of a pastor," Melanie said. "But that doesn't make him all bad. He wants the best for us kids. But time is pressing. We must go and meet him now."

"OK, we understand. But do come again. You'll be very welcome."

"OK, thanks, I intend to," Melanie replied as she shepherded Russell toward their car. Driving to the Castle Restaurant they both agreed about the friendliness of the people and that it had been a fascinating experience. Russell wondered if all the church services were like that.

Chapter 16. **Row Over Research**

CHRISTMAS AND THE NEW Year fled past, as they usually do. The holidays soon ended, and Benedict Hall opened up to the undergraduates again. Russell continued working on the *longiferase* project at both MoliMart and in his university lab. He, Zemki, and the team of technicians at MoliMart, had prepared a small library of *longiferase* variants. They had also set up several microorganism-based assays to test their effectiveness. As predicted, they found that *telomerase* catalyzed the docking of all but one of the variant *longiferase* enzymes with the telomere units of the microorganisms. Though it had extended the lifetimes of the microorganisms, it did so only by comparatively minor amounts. Careful analyses, carried out as the tests proceeded, suggested the problem was that the *longiferase* segments would then detach from the telomeres rather easily. They had tried adjusting the pH, ionic strength, and other parameters of the experiment, but with little improvement. None of Sir George's suggested remedies had helped. Zemki had nothing to offer. Dr. Irma's contribution was to keep insinuating that they must have made mistakes. The atmosphere in the labs was becoming more and more strained.

During the succeeding weeks, Russell decided to go back to the drawing board. He opened up his visualization software and spent long hours carefully examining the match of each *longiferase* variant with the telomere proteins. Comparing long lists of the types of bonding sites, he looked for hydrogen bonding, hydrophobic areas, and electrostatic interactions. Russell particularly searched for vacant areas and for any repulsive interactions, then computed models of hundreds of contact sites in the proteins, and drew up electrostatic potential surfaces of certain structural features. The problem was that the *longiferase* structures could easily shift between different shapes and conformations, forcing him to examine hundreds of conformations for each variant. Since everything he did was monitored and checked at Mo-liMart, he conducted all his computations on the main computer cluster at Excelsis so as to retain control of his ideas.

Dr. Vonvoigt, becoming increasingly impatient, frequently came to stare uncomprehendingly at the complex structures on Russell's computer screen, before urging him to do more practical experiments. "Theory and experiment are as inseparable as Hansel and Gretel," he told her. On another occasion she warned him that he should be doing experimental work like Zemki. Russell well knew Illovian had lost interest in the *lon-giferase* project shortly after the first few disappointing results. Certainly, Zemki was busy experimenting, but on a project of his own that he was secretive about. With a skeptical expression, Russell said, "The path of true research never did run smooth."

But Dr. Irma was a bureaucrat with no understanding of how research proceeded. She expected results to keep flowing out like products from a production line. "Why don't you check your experiments for contamina-tion and operator mistakes?" she kept asking him.

"I'm in process of re-designing," Russell would reply. "An ounce of inspiration is worth a pound of perspiration." Or he would say, "Good design always trumps random chance." Suddenly the relevance of his own words to neo-Darwinian evolution struck him. How, he wondered, could random chance mutations be responsible for the amazing complexity of all living things?

The unfriendly encounters with Dr. Irma recurred with irritating fre-quency, becoming more acrimonious as time progressed. Soon her tone became threatening. She began reminding him that his contract depended on satisfactory progress and stated that she saw little evidence of it. To try to get some relief, Russell approached Sir George, explaining to him that he was exploring *longiferase* conformations in search of adverse interactions. He asked him to talk to Dr. Vonvoight and try to get her off his back. After-ward her visits lessened, but the hostile atmosphere continued.

After weeks of painstaking searching, Russell found what he thought might be the problem. All the variant *longiferase*s readily adopted a troublesome low energy conformation. In that state, a small negatively charged group interacted repulsively with a negatively charged area on the telomeres. It seemed probable it led to the premature undocking. Before saying anything to the team about his conclusion, he decided to spend time thinking out a remedy. It occupied several more weeks such that Easter was soon approaching.

Meanwhile, life in Benedict Hall went on as usual. Winters tended to be mild in Columburgh, because of its closeness to the sea. On the days when chill easterly breezes blew, the sound of roaring surf would awaken the students early. Most mornings, as Russell was on his way to breakfast, Mrs. Maggs would greet him with a joke or proverb. Sensing things were not going well for him at his lab, she quipped, "Cheer up! Not everything on the Titanic was a failure. The swimming pool is still full to this day!" Russell made a wry face.

He attended Olympia's paleontology lectures every Wednesday and watched Ambi in action. Almost every week she came out with comments or questions that chipped away at Olympia's enthusiastic endorsement of evolution. During the lecture about the thousands of fossil bats, Ambi pointed out that so far paleontologists had never discovered any of their ancestors.

Olympia's illustrations of the amazing variety and size of dinosaur fossils were fascinating. When she spoke about feathered dinosaurs as intermediates with birds, Ambi interjected comments about the frauds found among the supposedly feathered Chinese fossil dinosaurs. On fossil flowering plants, Ambi said possible ancestors were unknown and the plants origins remained a mystery. On one memorable occasion Ambi actually agreed with Olympia! The discussion concerned fossils in the deepest Cambrian strata and the virtual absence of ancestral species in Precambrian sediments. Olympia admitted the sudden burst of complex life was something of a mystery. Ambi spoke up, agreeing that the Cambrian Explosion, when fossils from all the major taxa including kingdoms, phyla, classes, and orders, suddenly appeared, was a major puzzle for evolutionary biologists.

The lack of interest Slab, Veronica, and the bulk of the students attending the lectures showed in Ambi's comments puzzled Russell. It seemed they only paid attention to information that agreed with their prior beliefs and either rejected or ignored anything that conflicted with them. Most times, when Ambi raised her hand to ask a question, he heard groans or whispers of "Not again!" While overt hostility was rare, Ambi began receiving malicious and insulting emails that she forwarded to the University IT services.

Excitement built as the time for Olympia's field trip approached. It was designed to give first-hand experience of fossil hunting, retrieval, identification, and preservation. A month before Easter, Olympia circulated her information brochure. It disclosed that the trip was scheduled for three days in April during the Easter vacation. A Jurassic site in Wiltshire was known for exquisite fossils of fish, crustaceans, and cephalopoda, but its location was a closely guarded secret. The list of equipment each participant must bring included a geological pick, trowel, chisel, knife, tweezers, brush, and magnifying glass. The students could rent hard hats, goggles, and high visibility jackets. The brochure also mentioned that ankle injuries could be a problem, so it recommended strong boots with good ankle supports. Accommodations would be partly in huts and partly in tents, and most food would be cooked and consumed on site. Participants should bring their own treats and supplementary food. More than half the class signed up for the trip.

Chapter 17. **Lunch with the Amhursts**

RUSSELL LOOKED FORWARD TO his meetings with Ambi in the Bishop's Arms on Wednesdays. He admitted to himself that he felt strongly attracted to her. Clearly intelligent, she was a good listener, and was articulate and responsive. She laughed at his jokes and was good to look at. Was he in love with her? Although he'd had several girlfriends like Goldie in the past, Ambi seemed vastly different. He always got on so well with her. They were friends. Could a deeper relationship be possible? Aware that she was a conservative Christian, he wondered whether she just regarded him as a possible convert to her faith. Finally, he decided he didn't care. He liked her so much he was determined to keep on seeing as much of her as possible.

One Wednesday he made his way to the Bishop's Arms for a chat with her. It was a beautiful spring afternoon of pale sunshine, cotton-bud clouds, and gentle breezes. The surf was a soothing murmur on the distant beach. The trees were just opening new green shoots, and daffodils were coloring the gardens yellow. Cherry and Magnolia blossoms now adorned the University's green spaces. Meeting Ambi, Russell mentioned that he'd read the books she'd recommended by Kitchen and Bloomberg about the historical reliability of the Bible. They had convinced him not to trust internet assertions that the Bible was just a collection of folk tales. He said the archaeological evidence for the historical books in the Bible was very compelling. It had amazed him that even ancient civilizations such as the Hittites figured so frequently in the Bible. That hundreds of ancient artifacts demonstrated that events, places, and people in the Bible were historical. But he inquired, "The questions you ask Olympia seem to suggest you take the early chapters of Genesis seriously, too. Surely, these must be allegorical or poetical? You don't believe the Genesis accounts of a worldwide flood and creation are historical, too?"

"It all comes down to what you believe about God," she replied. "I don't think of God as just an old bearded superman living somewhere in the sky. It's difficult to understand, but He is not a material being such as we know. He isn't made of atoms and molecules, or flesh and blood, and he isn't either male or female. Being outside the material universe, He is not subject to the natural forces that govern us. In fact, these forces exist and act the way they do, because He wills them to act that way. God is a being of infinite power and infinite mind who brought all material things into existence. He created the universe and our world and finely tuned them to be ideal for human life."

"You're saying God is bigger than the Big Bang?"

"Yes. Absolutely! God is hugely interested in the material universe He made. And God is good. The source of all moral values, He loves good and right and hates bad and wrong. Given that He is infinite and all good, why would He take millions of years of horrible suffering, disease, and death, as evolution teaches, to make the human race? It would be so much better to create quickly and in the coordinated and well-designed way described in Genesis."

Russell had been trying to impress on Dr. Irma Vonvoigt the necessity for design in his research project, so the idea of design in the origin of the biological world resonated well with him. "You're feeding me lots of rich fare that I need to digest," he said. "I've plenty of questions. For example, what about all the fossils laid down in strata through hundreds of millions of years? But we'll be late for dinner at Benedict. We'd better get moving."

They hurried back to Benedict Hall through the evening sunshine, still talking. Ambi suggested that he come to her church that weekend. "My Dad will be talking about miracles. I think you'll be interested in what he has to say." Russell had been back to Ambi's church several times with Melanie, and had always enjoyed the experience, so he readily agreed.

On Friday, Ambi texted him saying that her parents had invited him for lunch after the church service. Russell responded that Melanie would be with him. Ambi replied that both would be welcome. That weekend, he picked up his sister in Dunchester. They bought a bouquet of yellow tulips and two bottles of lime and mint spritzer before driving to the Fidem Adventus Christi Church. The service followed the usual pattern. The choir sang well, and the children's responses during their story aroused affectionate laughter from the congregation. A reading from the Gospel of John described Jesus' healing of a man born blind and the subsequent investigation by the Jewish authorities. They had rejected the miracle, not because of any contrary evidence, but out of pure prejudice.

Pastor Amhurst's sermon began with the story of Irene MacDonald's remarkable recovery. Of Fredericton, New Brunswick, she had been diagnosed with rapidly progressing MS. A specialist had warned her it was terminal and that she had not long to live. Soon she couldn't move from her bed and was in such pain that she needed regular spinal injections. One Friday a friend told her God was going to heal her soon. Although understandably skeptical, a dream encouraged her, and she asked to be carried to church that Sunday. During prayer over her, her sense of feeling suddenly returned, and she regained full muscular strength and control over her body. Irene walked from the church and resumed her normal activities.

Pastor Amhurst said thousands of such medically authenticated miraculous healings were taking place in countries all round the world. He backed up his claim with a PowerPoint listing the title pages of books describing them. Then he went on to say that although most ordinary people accepted that miraculous and supernatural events took place, a highly secularized academic elite, favoured by the media, rejected them. The authorities in Jesus' day had denied His miracles, because they ran counter to their preconceptions. Today, Amhurst suggested, miracles are discounted or explained away, because they run counter to the prevailing naturalist worldview.

Amhurst said that people often claim that science has refuted miracles, or that the philosopher David Hume proved beyond doubt there could be no true miraculous events or happenings. He explained that Hume had claimed that miracles were violations of the laws of nature and, because such laws were regarded as inviolable and unchangeable, miracles must be impossible. It was exactly what Russell had heard many times from his father and at the Sceptics Society meetings. Then Amhurst pointed out the invalid circular reasoning in such an argument. Hume assumed that nature's laws were inviolable, but that decision itself was just as much in need of proof as the one about the invalidity of miracles. The conclusion was already present in the initial assumption. All the laws of nature are approximate, Amhurst emphasized, and only have ranges of applicability. Elevating such relationships to universal, unbreakable, and eternal laws greatly misrepresented them. They were actually limited and thus at best partial *descriptions* of the regularities one observed in nature.

As a result, they don't dictate what must always happen but merely describe normal undisturbed outcomes.

Christians, Amhurst explained, believe that during a miracle God reaches into the material universe from outside to introduce new circumstances or new power. Once the transfer has taken place, the normal laws take over again. He quoted the Oxford mathematician John Lennox, "What Christians are saying about the Resurrection of Jesus is not that he rose by a natural process that would violate the laws of nature. No. Christians claim Jesus rose because God injected enormous power and energy from outside the system. Now, unless you have evidence the system is totally closed, you cannot argue against the possibility of miracles."

On his PowerPoint, Amhurst displayed another quotation, this time from physicist and Anglican priest John Polkinghorne, who had written, "Science simply tells us that these events are against normal expectation. We knew this at the start. Science cannot exclude the possibility that, on particular occasions, God does particular, unprecedented things. After all, God is the ordainer of the laws of nature, not someone who is subject to them."

The evidence for the thousands of miracles happening in the modern world is overwhelming, Pastor Amhurst stressed. He then illustrated it with a story about a mother whose daughter was seriously ill. She hurriedly drove to pick up a prescription. When she got back to her car, she discovered that she had locked her keys inside. So, she sent up a silent prayer, "Dear God, I'm stuck, please, please send me some help." Almost immediately a rough-looking man on a motor bike stopped and asked if she needed a hand.

"Yes," she said. "My daughter is ill. I have the medicine, but I've locked my keys in the car. Can you open it?"

The man said, "Sure," and in less than a minute had the door open. The woman exclaimed, "Thank You, God, for sending such a nice man."

"Lady," the individual said, "I'm not a nice man. I was released from prison yesterday, where I did three years for car theft." Giving the man a hug, she said, "Thank You, God, for sending a professional." Laughter spread through the congregation.

"Of course, there are many false and fraudulent miracles out there," Amhurst continued. "So, caution is needed." After projecting a graphic of G. K. Chesterton's remark "Don't be so open-minded that your brains fall out!" he presented examples of false prophets and bogus miracles, adding, "In evaluating unusual events it is sensible to weigh the evidence and sift it carefully. Examine the character and reputation of the witnesses. Are they known as dependable, truthful, and honest people? The consistency of their evidence should be checked. Do they contradict themselves or one another in any way? Are they right about known places and events? What are their motives? Do they have anything to gain? Do circumstantial and indirect evidence agree and form a logical pattern? All this should be taken into consideration and then the reliability of the witnesses' evidence and how likely the miracle is to be true can be judged."

He finished by asking the congregation to imagine they had been there when Jesus healed the man born blind. "You would have heard the authorities question the man, his parents, and the bystanders. You would know they were decent folk with good characters who had nothing to gain from telling lies. Which side would you have been on? Would you have been with the sceptics? Would you have gone with the majority who assumed that because the experts rejected the miracle there must be something wrong with it? Would you have clung to secular naturalist preconceptions? Yes, be skeptical," he said, "but be moderate in your skepticism. Don't allow it to lead to spiritual blindness that blocks you from the promptings of God through Scripture, through your conscience, through what you hear from the speaking or writing of other Christians. Some of the preachers and prophets you may encounter on the internet are false, but by no means all."

His final thought for the congregation was, "Would you have let the evidence speak for itself and agreed with the once blind beggar that a mighty miracle had indeed occurred? That the miracle was a profound witness to Jesus as Son of God and to His mission of giving life and life in abundance to all who believe?"

As he and Melanie drove to Ambi's home, Russell mused over what he had heard. Being a scientist, he knew something of the limited applicability of the laws of nature. It was true, he thought to himself, they were no more than descriptions of so far observed regularities in nature. He knew they didn't dictate what must happen. Outside intervention could lead to radically different outcomes. Amhurst had raised serious doubts about the validity of David Hume's arguments. Miracles could be real after all. Russell determined to check out the miracle books Amhurst had alluded to.

The Amhurst home was a moderate-sized, stone-built house set in modest gardens in a respectable suburb of Dunchester. Ambi and her mother admitted them to the hallway which was floored with light wood and had white painted walls. Framed pictures depicted scenes from nature. Oak panel doors led to various rooms, and a carpeted stairway, with fancy wooden banisters, disappeared upstairs. Vases and pots of flowers were everywhere. Melanie and Russell presented their flowers and the bottles of juice they had brought. Thanking them, Ambi led them to the drawing room. There, she introduced them to her father and her younger sister, Rosalinda. Daniel Smith, whom they'd met before, was already present.

After they accepted soft drinks and took seats, Russell noticed two bookcases full of books in the room. Soon he discovered books were stacked everywhere in the house. A glass-topped case in one corner contained a collection of old coins. Soft classical music played in the background. Pastor John Amhurst turned out to be a friendly and affable man as he welcomed them to his home. He said Ambi had told him a bit about them, but he asked Melanie what her interests were. She happily told him about her job with her father's construction firm and that she was studying management. Delighted at the opportunity of relating to a new audience about her recent visit to the Fidem Health and Wellbeing Institute, Melanie launched into a description of the fitness classes, the hill walks, and Dr. Regius's presentations. It turned out that John Amhurst knew the physician. "We sometimes invite him to give talks at the church," he said.

"Have you ever had a miracle happen to you?" Russell asked.

"Oh, yes," he responded. "When I was studying to become a pastor, archaeology was an important part of my course work. I wanted to go on an expedition to Jericho in the Jordan Valley of the West Bank to see for myself if the walls had really fallen down as recorded in Exodus in the Bible. The cost of the trip was twelve hundred pounds, but I had only been able to raise eight hundred from holiday jobs and savings. Time was running out, so one morning I prayed for God to send me the money if He wanted me to be part of the expedition. That same day an envelope addressed to me arrived through the post containing eight fifty-pound notes, the exact sum I needed. I never discovered who sent it. The only note with the money just said, "From a well-wisher!"

"That's amazing! And did you find that the ancient wall of Jericho had really fallen?"

"Emphatically yes! I saw the debris of the fallen walls and extensive burning of the city that three sets of archaeologists had uncovered. Archaeologist Kathleen Kenyon had dated this destruction to long before the time of Joshua and the Exodus on the basis of pottery comparisons. But it turned out she had overlooked key evidence. More recent reassessments place the event squarely at the time the Bible indicated. I've since given many faith-building talks including this evidence."

Rosalinda had abundant hair like her sister's, though a lighter shade of brown. But she had the same bright intelligent eyes. At first she was too shy to say anything, only staring at the tall and good-looking Russell. Daniel made her blush by frowning pointedly at her and saying sharply, "It's rude to stare!" Russell judged she would be eight or nine years old. To draw attention away from her, he said kindly, "Staring is nicer than glaring! Rosalinda is a pretty name, but it's quite a mouthful. Tell me, do your friends shorten it?"

"Yes," she said shyly, "most people call me Rosie."

Just then Mrs. Amhurst appeared and invited them to the dining room for lunch. It was quite a feast, starting with lentil carrot and coriander soup with either seeded, granary, or rye bread. A delicate cheese soufflé then followed, accompanied by boiled Jersey Royal potatoes, garden peas, carrots, and salad. The dessert was a homemade apple pie with rainbow sorbet. Russell asked who had made the apple pie, and Ambi told him she and Rosie had joined forces in baking it. Mrs. Amhurst requested that Russell open the bottles of spritzer. Rosie watched in fascination as he peeled back the silver paper, untwisted the wires from the cork, then eased it gently out. She jumped with fright when he pointed the bottle toward the ceiling and the cork flew out with a sharp bang and bounced around. After the meal, Russell and Melanie warmly thanked Mrs. Amhurst for such delicious fare and offered to help with washing up. She thanked them, but said not to bother, because they had a dishwasher and would see to that later.

They all moved to the drawing room where Ambi and Rosie served coffee and tea. When Mrs. Amhurst asked him about his research, Russell told them a little about MoliMart and how he was trying to find a way of increasing human longevity. John Amhurst said light-heartedly, "Then we are pretty much in the same business! We seek the same goal, but from quite different directions!"

"How do you work that out?" Russell asked.

"Well, Christ said that He had come to give life and give it more abundantly. He meant 'more abundantly' in the fullest possible sense. His mission was to restore to humankind the eternal life they had lost in Eden. My Christian mission is to offer the good news that this everlasting life is available to anyone who believes and accepts Christ. We called our daughter Ambrosine, which means 'immortal,' as a symbol of our commitment to this."

"I'd never thought about Christianity that way," Russell said thoughtfully. "I'd heard it was all about convicting people of sin and urging them to lead better lives or face hellfire. I guess your way to eternal life is top down. I'm hoping my way to longevity won't amount to bootstrapping up!"

"A remedy for sin is another aspect of Christianity. But it's not so much convicting of sin as getting people to recognize it in themselves and realize they can only do something about it with help from above."

Rosie was getting a bit restless as the adults kept talking. Daniel was starting to look disapprovingly at her. Noticing it, Russell turned to her and asked, "Do you have a hobby? What do you like doing?"

Perking up, she said, "I love reading and listening to stories."

Russell smiled. "Everyone loves stories, including me."

"Do you know a happy story to tell me?" she asked innocently.

"Now Rosie, don't be saucy," her mother interjected. "Mr. Marshall is a scientist. He hasn't time for little girl's stories."

But Russell motioned for Rosie to sit near him. "Once upon a time," he began, "there was a little girl who lived on a farm. Fruits grew on the orchard trees and fields of corn swayed in the breeze. Bees drew honey from flowers that drank up the showers. She was a very forgetful girl, so her parents called her Forgetorella. Her dad always told her, 'Don't stray out on the road,' but one day as she was playing by the farmhouse gate, she forgot and set off down the road. The sun was shining, the sky was blue, the breeze was gentle, and adventure was calling, she knew. She came to a fork in the road and recited, 'East or West, right is always best:' so she turned right."

"As she was walking along, she came across a black stone and was just going to kick it, when the stone said, 'Don't kick me.' So, she picked it up and put it in her pocket. She walked further and came to a shiny silver coin. As she was just about to kick it, it said, 'Don't kick me.' So, she picked it up and slipped it into her pocket. After she had walked a long way further, she saw a juicy red apple on the road. Just as she was about to kick it, the apple said, 'Don't kick me!' So, she picked it up and put it in her pocket."

"When she came to another fork in the road, she again recited, 'East or West, right is always best:' and took the right fork. By now it was lunch time, the sun was hot, and she was hungry and thirsty. But she couldn't remember the way home."

"Could you have directed her home?" Russell asked Rosie.

"Oh yes! Just take two left turns."

"Correct. But Forgetorella had forgotten! She walked on and on, then came across a van selling food. Hungry, she went up to the man and asked him for something to eat."

"'Show me your money,' he said."

"'I'm sorry, but I don't have any. Please can you spare me something,' she pleaded."

"'No dough, off you go,' he said. But just at that moment the silver coin flew out of her pocket and landed on the counter. The man picked it up and gave her a cheese and tomato sandwich, a pink ice cream, and a carton of apple juice."

"She soon ate this all up and walked on to another fork in the road. 'East or West, right is always best,' and once again she took the right fork. She felt very lost and was looking puzzled. Just then a rough and dirty man rushed out of a door and seized her arm."

"'You come with me,' he said angrily. 'You're going to wash and clean and cook for me from now on!' and he dragged her toward his house."

"But just then the stone shot out of her pocket and hit the man on his forehead. Stumbling back, he let go of Forgetorella's arm. She ran away as fast as she could and came to another fork in the road. 'East or West, right is always best,' she chanted and took the right fork again."

"Round the corner she saw a huge angry pig rushing toward her. A farmer was chasing it, and he called to her to stop the animal. But the pig was much bigger than her. *How can I stop an angry pig?* she thought. But just then the juicy red apple bounced out of her pocket and rolled toward the pig. Now if there is one thing pigs really like, it's juicy apples! So, the pig stopped and started to eat the apple. The farmer rushed up and put a rope on the pig to lead it home."

"Really grateful to Forgetorella, he said, 'I never thought a little girl like you could stop my pig! What can I do for you?'"

"'I'm lost,' she explained, 'and I want to go home.'"

"'What's your name?' he asked. 'Where do you live'?" But Forgetorella couldn't remember her name or where she lived!"

"Looking closely at her, the farmer said, 'I think I recognize you! Aren't you Forgetorella! You live on the farm next to mine. Come this way!' Soon she saw her own front gate and rushed back to her parents. From then on, she remembered things better and lived happily ever after."

Everyone gently clapped as Russell finished. "I know why she got home!" Rosie exclaimed. "She took four right turns, so they circled her back to near her home!"

"That's right! But I think there was a little magic in the air that day," Russell responded.

Turning to Pastor Amhurst, he started to ask about the coin display he had noticed, but Ambi broke in, suggesting that they should go for a walk while the sun was shining. She, Melanie, Rosie, and Russell went for a brisk walk round the nearby park, and then Melanie and Russell took their leave.

In the kitchen, the Amhurst womenfolk agreed that it had been a lovely occasion. In the uninhibited way of the very young, Rosie announced, "I love Russell! He tells super stories!" Her mother agreed. She had liked the kind-hearted way he had behaved toward her Rosie and the generous thought of bringing her flowers, silently contrasting it with Daniel who was rather cold, apt to be controlling, and rarely gave gifts. Ambi nodded. Happy to have Russell as a friend, she was grateful that, after the paleontology lectures, he always came to stand with her. Just his presence eased much of the unpleasantness of the frightening emails she had been receiving. His support had been reassuring. She knew that, though he might not agree with everything she said, he fully backed her right to ask questions.

Chapter 18. **The Fossil Field Trip**

RUSSELL HAD SPENT MANY days with his visualization software, searching for a way forward in the *longiferase* project. He was convinced there must be some means of preventing the repulsive interaction with the telomere proteins. What was needed, he thought, was a co-factor that would interact with the *longiferase* variants and prevent them from adopting the problematic conformation. But the co-factor must not block the docking process. He began searching for comparatively small biomolecules that would make at least two hydrogen bonds to the variant *longiferase*s and would thereby restrict their internal motions so as to exclude the unwanted structure. Eventually he found about six possible co-factors, including one that looked especially promising. By now he'd learned not to confide anything with Sir George if he wanted credit for his ideas. Instead, he arranged to give a presentation at the next regular meeting of the whole research group.

It took place in a biochemistry tutorial room at Excelsis on the Thursday before Good Friday. For the occasion, Irma Vonvoigt, Zemki Illovian, and the rest of the MoliMart team, had been invited to join. Using PowerPoint, Russell displayed the key structural maps showing the repulsive interaction from the low energy *longiferase* conformation. There was a dismayed silence as he explained that it was probably responsible for the premature undocking. When he paused, an angry Dr. Irma broke in, saying, "So the whole project was doomed from the start! We should have been informed of this at MoliMart before we committed all our resources."

"Hold on there," Sir George interrupted. "No need to jump to unwarranted conclusions. Research is always an uncertain business. It's never possible to cover every eventuality right from the word go."

Resuming his presentation, Russell stated that he thought he had found a way of getting around the problem. Then he screened graphics unwrapping his idea of restricting the conformational space of the *longiferase* variants. Could they be induced to weakly bond with a co-factor in such a way as to prevent them from developing the unfavorable structural shape? He then showed more graphics of the *longiferase* variants in association with five of the six possible co-factors he had identified. But he did not mention the sixth co-factor, the one he thought most promising, reserving that as his own part of the project. Also, he said nothing about several further insights his in-depth analysis had led to. Instead, he suggested that the way forward was for the group either to find sources for the first five co-factors or to synthesize them. Then the docking of the *longiferase* variants with the telomere proteins could be tested in the presence of those co-factors. The mood in the room shifted rapidly from pessimism to optimism. Most of the anger faded from Dr. Irma's face. Some group members offered possible modifications to the co-factor structures. Others thought they knew where to source some of them. They rapidly agreed to proceed along the lines that Russell had indicated as soon as Easter was over.

Russell and Melanie attended the Easter Sunday service at the Fidem Adventus Christi Church. He especially enjoyed the wonderful harmonies of Handel's Messiah. Ambi sang "Panis Angelicus" with power and pathos. While those aspects of Easter had delighted him, the cruelty and injustice of the crucifixion story had repelled him. Questions hammered in his mind. If Jesus were God, why would He subject himself to such pain and humiliation? If it was just a matter of dealing with sin, why didn't God simply pardon sinners? And were there a need to abolish evil, why didn't God just exterminate Satan and his hosts? He determined to get Ambi's views on his questions, but meanwhile he was preoccupied with getting ready for Prof. Olympia's field trip. It was due to start on the Tuesday, so Russell began collecting the equipment, supplies, and clothing he would need.

He gathered all the gear Olympia had specified. In addition, he loaded his backpack with a sleeping mat, pillow, nightwear, toiletries, a change of clothes, a flashlight and spare batteries, two pairs of thin vinyl gloves, some sterile sample tubes, some packs of fruit energy bars, and some chocolate. Early Tuesday morning he joined the group of about twenty students waiting for two minibuses outside the biology theater. Prof. Olympia, with two senior postgraduate students to help with instruction, would travel separately in a Range Rover pulling a camping trailer. They loaded mountains of gear into the buses, then set off for Wiltshire, arriving at the site in the afternoon. Close to the site was a permanent facility with showers, toilets, and a meeting room. Prof. Olympia parked the trailer, where she would be sleeping, next to the facility. The campsite, which was a short walk from the actual fossil site, was equipped with two-person tents, camp beds, sleeping bags, and the other gear they had rented.

On arrival, Olympia gathered all the students for an introductory talk. She welcomed them all, said the weather forecast was mixed, but that they should get plenty of fossil hunting time. Introducing the two postgrads, she explained their role. She emphasized the need for care and safety and asked the students to all watch out for one another. "Any indiscipline will result in the culprits being sent home immediately," she stressed. "I know you can't wait to see the campsite and your sleeping arrangements, so I'm sending you now to check it out. Choose your tents and get your living arrangements settled. But don't go to the actual fossil site before re-convening for a further lecture here at the facility meeting room at 6 o'clock."

There was a general rush to the tent area, followed by a lot of joshing and giggling about who was going to share which tent with whom. The tents were widely spread in a rough circle around a fire pit. Two large barbeque grills were positioned off to one side. Russell and Lawrence had got together. They had both noticed that Slab and his cronies had brought multiple cans of lager, as well as full hip flasks with them. Slab would share with Jonah Jeffries and Nollum with Billy Howard. They set up near Veronica who was bunking with Anna Bellamy.

"I want to be well away from Slab when he's drinking," Lawrence whispered to Russell. "He's dangerous! He's a judo champion, and he's known to have broken his opponents' arms and legs!" They arranged their tent far from Slab and near to Ambi who was sharing with Shuchun. As Russell and Lawrence got their stuff arranged, it crossed Russell's mind that Slab might attempt some pilfering, peeping, or bullying of the girls. Having brought along a couple of padlocks to keep the tent flaps as secure as possible, he gave the spare one to Ambi, explaining what it was for.

At 6:00 p.m. the students all gathered in the facility. Prof. Olympia joined them, wearing figure-hugging blue jeans and a short denim top, revealing her shapely midriff. "First things first!" she began. "About food. We will be having simple food that we prepare ourselves. There are plenty of hamburgers and buns. For those who prefer them, we've even brought veggie-burgers. We have sliced bread, butter, cheese, ham, and even jars of strawberry jam. For dessert there are apples, oranges, and bananas. You will find stacks of firewood by the facility, but we have permission to gather more from the nearby woods. The facility has folding tables you can use to prepare things. All litter must be gathered up and put in the black bin bags. Go to it, and let's get the show on the road."

Olympia was too much of a feminist to divide the work between males and females. However, as almost always happens, the guys set up the tables, got a large fire going in the pit, and lit the charcoal briquettes in the two barbeque units. The girls unwrapped the food and arranged it on the tables. They added cartons of apple, orange, and grape juice as well as milk. After spreading the bread with butter, they handed the burgers to the guys for grilling. Their equipment included a butane burner, and the girls filled the kettle and set it on to boil for tea and coffee. In surprisingly little time everything was ready. Prof. Olympia called for everyone to fill a paper cup with juice. Holding hers aloft, she declared, "Here's to successful fossil hunting!" Everyone echoed her words. Slab had carefully grilled a burger which he presented to her on a paper plate. When she asked for Bar-Be-Que sauce, he hurried to get her the bottle. The rest of the students helped themselves and grouped round the fire to eat and drink.

As soon as eating waned, Russell assisted the postgrads to collect all the litter in the bin bags. Prof. Olympia summoned everyone back to the main facility, saying their time there was short, so they must make best possible use of it. She circulated copies of a geological map divided into ten large sections indicating the area where each would be collecting.

"Know the lay of the land," she explained. "You will work in pairs, each assigned to the section I've given you. It's easy to miss things, so if time permits, we will swap sections to cross-check the search. This site's not easily accessible, it's in a remote spot with only a few farms nearby. Not many fossil hunters have been here before, and we are the first this year, so there are good prospects for interesting finds. This locale has Jurassic sedimentary strata interspersed with metamorphic and igneous layers. Look for fossils in the sandstone, mudstone, and shale strata marked on your maps. Ammonites, bivalves and protozoans are the index fossils for Jurassic strata, so watch for those." Noting that while Jurassic strata did sometimes contain dinosaur fossils, it was unlikely they would find any at this particular site, but, she concluded, "In fossil hunting you never know!"

One of the postgraduate students gave them a short talk and demonstration of the best ways of using the geological pick, trowel, chisel, and knife. "If you find any interesting or well-preserved fossils, don't dig them up yourself," she cautioned. "Call one of us, and we will gather everyone to demonstrate the best way of retrieving and getting specimens back to the lab." She told them to make careful notes, take photographs from several angles, and mark the locations of any discoveries on the maps they had received. Dismissed, the students headed back to the tents. They gathered round the embers of the fire and continued talking and laughing far into the night.

Breakfast next morning consisted of smoky sausages, cereals, and milk, with bread, butter, and jam washed down with tea, coffee, or juice. The students tried to toast the bread by holding it near the flames on sharpened sticks but mainly got smoke-blackened or burnt results.

Prof. Olympia and her two postgraduates inspected their footwear, then dispatched them all to their allotted sections. The search area was about twenty square miles of undulating scrub-covered moorland with many sandy areas, rocky outcrops, and hollows. Taking their map, water bottles, picks, trowels and chisels, Russell and Lawrence headed to their allotted section. They had divided it on their map into manageable sized squares and now marked off the first square with string. Then they started carefully searching, advancing side by side, overturning vegetation, shifting rocks, breaking any that took their fancy, and digging with their picks. The first hour went by quickly but then it became hard back-breaking work, and they were glad for the water they had brought. They found several attractive stones that Russell thought would polish up well. Although encouraged by finding a couple ammonites which they bagged, they were too small and of too poor quality for them to show Prof. Olympia. From time to time they heard shouts from other students. Since they were not summoned over, they concluded the finds were not important enough for the full retrieval treatment.

When they walked back for a sandwich and fruit lunch, they found the others excitedly comparing their finds. Almost everyone had found something. Several had small ammonites and several types of bivalves. One pair had found pieces of fossilized wood. Prof. Olympia and the postgrads brought out examples to show from their own fossil collections. It appeared that one of the bivalves could be from the *Carditida* order and another from the order *Mytilida*. The fossil wood was a species of pine. A light drizzle started in the afternoon, but the students were undeterred. Having seen the various finds, they now had a better idea of what to search for. Discoveries came thick and fast, and by the end of the afternoon they all returned and set them out on the tables. Most of them were more ammonites and bivalves, but an exciting one was a small, mineralized crustacean.

The rain thickened for a while that evening, so Prof. Olympia showed them videos of previous fossil hunts, including one from the famous Hell Creek Formation in Montana where paleontologists had unearthed numerous dinosaur bones. She and the postgraduates then screened a PowerPoint to show how to document and retrieve a valuable fossil. First, one laid a grid over the fossil so that all the original positions of the bones could be plotted on grid paper. Then the postgrads showed how to make a plaster jacket to hold the fossil together, how to undercut it and flip it over to cap the underside with more plaster. The fossil could then be safely transported to the lab. The rain eventually let up, and they all adjourned to the tent area to make themselves another barbecue meal. Prof. Olympia related tales of hair-raising near accidents on previous fossil trips. One of the students produced a guitar and played popular songs that many joined in singing. As soon as Olympia retired to her trailer, Slab and Nollum brought out their cans of larger and started drinking. Most of the students were tired out after a full day outdoors and soon lay down in their tents to sleep.

The next morning at breakfast, Ambi told Russell she was grateful to him for the padlock, because someone had been trying to get into her tent. The padlock had stopped them. It was the last full day of collecting, so they all dispersed quickly to their sites. As before, Prof. Olympia and the post-graduates set off to patrol the area, using field glasses to keep an eye on the students. Russell and Lawrence had been carefully systematic, and by lunch-time were approaching the central area of their section when they came across a dry clay-like stratum about two feet thick. Breaking into it with their picks, they encountered a profusion of well-preserved ammonite, fish, and crustacean fossils. Immediately they shouted for Prof. Olympia who joined them and appeared quite excited about their find. She helped them trace the course of the clay stratum as it crossed three of the other students' sections. Then summoning all the students to observe, she, together with the postgrads, selected a beautiful *Lepidotes* fossil fish, documented its location, and demonstrated how to remove it using a plaster cast.

Russell came across several small coleoids (squid-like creatures). It amazed him to see how well preserved they were. Soft parts were still visible, showing muscle fibers and blood vessels. As a biochemist he well knew, from disastrous losses of enzymes and tissues in the lab, how rapidly such tissues degraded. He showed the specimens to everyone and asked

Prof. Olympia how old they were. To his astonishment, she said they had come from Jurassic strata about 160 million years old.

"How on earth can such delicate biological structures survive millions of years?" he asked.

"Yes, it's surprising," she admitted. "But soft tissues and even proteins are being found in more and more fossils from throughout the geological column. There must be especially efficient preservation modes that operate in such strata. One proposal is that iron particles cause cross-linking of the proteins, so extending their lifetimes."

Russell and Ambi had both studied chemistry and both looked skeptical.

"Iron compounds generate free radicals via a process known as the Fenton reaction," Ambi commented. "They are highly reactive and cause more damage by oxidation."

"Well, I don't know how the preservation happens," Olympia said. "But science will soon discover the answer."

"Let's preserve some of these coleoids," Russell suggested. "I have access to analytical instruments that could tell us if there are any actual proteins still existing in them." Although Olympia looked doubtful, she agreed. Russell asked if it would be worthwhile having some of the specimens radiocarbon dated.

"Of course not!" Prof. Olympia said derisively. "They're 160 million years old! All the radiocarbon will have decayed away millions of years ago. They are completely radiocarbon dead! It would be a complete waste of resources."

Russell carefully documented and photographed the location of a coleoid fossil, encased it in plaster, and added it to the general collection. In view of Prof. Olympia's skepticism, he slipped on his thin vinyl lab gloves and extracted two more of the small crustacean fossils, putting them in the personal specimen tubes he had brought with him. Everyone now returned for lunch. Afterward, Prof. Olympia suggested all the students should focus on searching the clay stratum. It contained the most fossils and would be the best use of their remaining time at the site. Everyone started on a different part of the stratum, splitting the thin laminations, and digging down as deep as they could go with their available tools. All of them were delighted to bring back to the facility excellent fossil specimens of various species of crustaceans and fish.

Noticing everyone was getting tired of burgers, Prof. Olympia sent one of the postgrads in the Range Rover to the nearest town to buy pizza. It was nearly cold when it arrived, but they all enjoyed a slice or two. They spent much of the evening arranging, cataloguing, and packaging their fossil collection for transport back to Columburgh, and in writing up their notes. Tired but triumphant, they gathered round the fire with paper cups of tea or coffee to discuss the day's finds. Russell shared the dark chocolate he had brought, and everyone relished a couple of squares. Others exchanged treats and more music was played.

After Prof. Olympia retired to her camping trailer, Slab and his group made serious inroads into the alcohol they had brought. Soon they were getting loud and boisterous. Russell thought he heard the words, "I dare you!" but couldn't make out what it was about. Most of the students retired to their tents for the night. Veronica was not fond of Slab when he was in a dangerous mood, so she and Anna walked back to the washrooms to prepare for the night. That was the signal for Slab to get up and stride round to Ambi's tent. Grabbing a bunch of her hair, he started pulling her toward the nearby woods, announcing, "I've warned you several times to lay off Olympia. Now I'm going to give it to you! Stop struggling, or I'll cut off all your hair!"

Furious, Russell jumped up and grabbed Slab's arm. "Let go this instant," he barked.

"You stay out of this, or you'll get seriously hurt! Besides, she's been begging for this. She really wants it. Out of my way, or I'll wreck you!"

Russell chopped the edge of his hand down on Slab's arm, forcing him to release Ambi's hair. Quickly picking up a large stone from the fire enclosure, she stood watching.

"Right, you've asked for this. You're dead," Slab shouted. "We'll fight, and the girl belongs to the winner."

"You're such a clown!" Russell mocked, enraging Slab further. Ambi watched tensely as the two circled round each other. While both were tall and strong looking, she feared for Russell, knowing Slab's judo reputation, and kept her stone in readiness. Slab advanced and retreated, making professional feints left and right. Suddenly, he pivoted on his right leg, and rapidly rotating his entire body, ended with a whirlwind left kick to Russell's throat. It was a killer blow, designed to do permanent damage.

But Russell had trained his reflexes during countless hours in the gym. Easily anticipating Slab's kick, he seized his foot by toe and heel and twisted sharply in the direction of the kick. There was a sickening crack. The momentum of the kick, reinforced by Russell's own momentum, spun Slab face down into the ground with a crash. He stayed there, unmoving. The fight was over that quickly.

Ambi dropped her stone, burst into tears, and sank to the ground. Going over to her, Russell put his arm round her. "It's over," he said. "He's not going to get up from that." As she leaned on him and rested her head on his shoulder, her sobs gradually subsided.

Slab's sudden defeat stunned Nollum and his other friends. They gathered round him in a dismayed huddle. "You murderous bastard! You've killed him!" Nollum accused Russell, forgetting to hiss in his consternation. "You'll get life for this!"

"Nonsense," Russell retorted, gently leading Ambi to her tent where Shuchun put an arm round her. Bending over Slab and finding his pulse normal, he said, "I've dislocated or broken his left knee, and he stunned himself falling. He'll be in considerable pain when he wakes up. One of you go tell Prof. Olympia that Slab has had an accident. He was demonstrating a judo trick when he tripped, fell, and stunned himself."

Prof. Olympia arrived and surveyed the scene. "I hope you guys haven't been fighting," she said. By now Slab was coming around, groaning dreadfully, and clutching his knee. Olympia made him swallow two ibuprofen tablets from the first-aid kit, got his friends to wrap him in a blanket in case of shock, and had them carry him to the back seat of the Range Rover. Then she deputized one of the postgrads to drive him to the nearest Accident and Emergency facility. Looking round at all the students who had gathered, she announced, "The excitement's over. I suggest you all turn in for the night. We have a long journey tomorrow."

Russell went over to Ambi's tent to see if she was OK. Although rather shaken and her head still hurt from where Slab had grabbed her hair, she assured him that she would be OK and just needed a good night's sleep. After telling her good night, he headed to his own tent.

The talk at breakfast next day was all about both the fight and the superb fossils they had collected. Veronica arrived and was just asking where Slab was, when Prof. Olympia announced that she had phoned the hospital. Though Slab was comfortable, his knee injury was serious, and he would need to see a specialist. He would remain at the hospital at least for the coming weekend. Learning what had happened, Veronica tried to phone Slab. Getting no answer, she sent him a sympathetic text message.

Chattering away, the students cleared and cleaned the campsite and loaded the minibuses with all their gear and the fossil specimens.

Chapter 19. **Fair and Foul in Conflict**

RUSSELL SAT NEXT TO Ambi on the return journey. They swapped their thoughts about the events of the night before.

"Are you OK today?" he asked. "I hope you're not too traumatized after Slab's vicious attack?"

"I can't wait for a proper shower to wash all trace of his horrible hands out of my hair! You were the Prince to my Rapunzel. You were my knight in shining armor yesterday. Slab was going to vent his spleen by brutalizing me! I would have been lost without you. I don't think anyone else could have flattened him. I can't thank you enough. Did you train in martial arts?"

"No, but I work out regularly and include routines to sharpen my reflexes. Fast reflexes are a key advantage in self-defense. Slab wanted to hurt you by damaging your beautiful hair! He's a lost soul, really. You know, I think violence is his admission he can't defend his origins beliefs with reason."

"Yes! It seems that anyone who opposes evolutionary orthodoxy finds themselves subjected to constant bullying. Now this! For me Slab turned cancel culture cruel."

"Perhaps he thought behaving like a cave man would persuade you that we are descended from apes?" Russell suggested with a smile.

"Ha, Ha! He only persuaded me of the baneful influence of the 'survival of the fittest' mindset! Because he's big and strong he thinks he has a natural right to spread his DNA as widely as possible! Actually, he persuaded me that the cosmic conflict between good and evil reaches every corner of this world; even Excelsis University. I was nearly its latest victim."

"What do you mean by 'cosmic conflict?'"

"The concept of a continuing struggle between good and evil runs all the way through Scripture. It started in celestial regions when a powerful angelic being called Lucifer or Satan, because of pride and self-exaltation, rebelled against God. The Bible often symbolizes him as a serpent or dragon. He persuaded other angelic beings to join him by claiming God's rule was unjust, unfair, and restricting. The conflict spread to earth when, in Eden, our first ancestors, Adam and Eve, were allured by Satan's words, and by eating the forbidden fruit, aligned themselves with him, God's archenemy."

"What makes you think this is real and that such a war is raging today?"

"Well, the cosmic conflict theme explains much about the state of the world we live in. The perplexing mixture of good and bad we see in history and in the world today. The fact that almost everyone believes in peace and justice, almost everyone has a deep longing for things to be put right, but it's never achieved. Not between nations, between communities, or even within families. Injustice, brutality, and malice directed against the innocent, go on year in year out despite all the best political solutions, despite all the progressive educational programs, despite all the enlightened training. Slab just gave an apt demonstration of this. What's more, echoes of this conflict appeared in corrupted forms in many ancient pagan religions. The same theme has surfaced in different guises down the ages. I'm sure you know of Milton's poem *Paradise Lost* which narrates it in epic style. It's found in modern western culture through books and stories such as Tolkien's *Lord of the Rings* trilogy and C.S. Lewis's seven *Narnia* books. Blockbuster films such as the *Star Wars* series also depict it in a veiled way. Knowing that there is a battle going on, encouraged by unseen forces, helps us understand the mixture of good and evil that pervades the natural world."

Russell thought a moment. "That's interesting, but why would a good God, and one that's also all powerful, let such a conflict continue? Why doesn't he just step in, destroy this angel, and put an end to evil?"

"God never treats us as just expendable pawns to be maneuvered or exploited as objects. He created us as free moral agents, with the freedom to choose how we behave, even to rebel, if we so wish. Lucifer claims that God denies such freedom to choose. That He is arbitrary and dictatorial. That we can't trust Him. You hear those same slanders being bandied about in the world today. Not only did God grant us the freedom to rebel, but He also permitted Satan the opportunity to spread his slanders and deceits. The outcome is the morally and physically blighted world we see today. If God simply annihilated those who challenged or opposed Him, He would immediately confirm all the worst fears of doubters and the uncommitted.

Suppose an earthly president was charged with corruption? Would annihilating all his accusers convince everyone of his innocence?"

"OK, I see your point. But how does God go about establishing what He is really like then?"

"He chooses to provide *evidence* to all created beings. On one hand, evidence of the disastrous results that following Satan's policies bring. On the other, evidence of His own true character by words, actions, and deeds. He intervenes from time to time, but always with great care, adapting His approach to meet differing circumstances as well as individuals in ways they can understand. His supreme action to demonstrate His character of love, and to expose Satan's malice, was to Himself become a member of the human race. He was born as a babe in Bethlehem and lived among us, demonstrating His love and sharing in the human plight. Satan revealed his totally evil character by seeking to destroy God. The totality of God's love for humanity was made plain in His willingness to even die on their behalf. That's the real message of the Easter story that we presented in our service last weekend."

"OK. I can see how that concept helps explain the state the world is in. But the idea we are caught up in a real but unseen conflict lasting untold ages is a scary one! Will it ever end? Does it go on forever? What could be the final outcome?"

"In the end, God will be vindicated against all the accusations brought against Him. Scripture, particularly in the book of Revelation, makes plain that the death and resurrection of Christ settled the final outcome. At the appropriate time, all evil agencies will be destroyed. God will achieve His original purpose to create a universe of love and harmony. Those who have faith in God, and simply accept Christ as Lord, will live forever in this beautiful Eden-like place."

"Did your parents choose your name, Ambrosine, as a sign they plan to be part of this eternal kingdom?"

"Yes! I'm kind of a walking signpost, a living, breathing symbol. It's hard to live so people interpret my symbol correctly! But I'm certainly trying! What about you, Russell? What do you believe in? What do you see in your future?"

"I used to believe there was no future for me or for the world. I could live with that, just taking satisfaction from the simple pleasures of life and expecting nothing more. But the unprincipled behavior of other atheists towards me personally, and in the wider context of international affairs, makes me think atheism is an arid and unlovely ideology. What I've learned in this paleontology course, the questions you've asked, and the lack of plausible answers, has made me seriously question secular naturalism and its evolutionary backing. As a result, I'm becoming skeptical of what I was taught in school and college about Scripture being all myth and fiction. I'm trying to have an open mind and follow the evidence wherever it leads."

"I'm happy to hear that! You can't do better! If there's anything I can do to help, do let me know. I can recommend more books and videos."

"OK. Thanks. I'm already following up on tons of leads and references."

She frowned and was silent a moment. "I've been getting vile and threatening emails recently. I'm wondering if now they will stop."

"You think they may have come from Slab?"

"It's possible, but it might be one of his cronies. I saw you picked up on the significance of the preserved soft tissues in those crustacean fossils. One thing that often happens is that such evidence disappears. Lab technicians and museum curators consider such fossils as unimportant or uninteresting. They don't fit in with their evolutionary scheme. Relegated to back drawers or dusty cupboards in the basement, they eventually get cleared out or lost. Occasionally the evidence is deliberately destroyed. I hope that's not going to happen to the fossils you collected."

"I saved two good specimens in my own tubes. I'm going to analyze them for preserved proteins. We all have to write final reports about the field trip. I'll include this evidence in mine."

The buses delivered them back to Columburgh that afternoon. The students lugged the crates of fossils to the paleontology lab. The technician there, Jan Parrott, received them and started the task of cleaning and preparing them for the end of course exhibition.

Chapter 20. **The Fossil Exhibition.**

THE NEXT MORNING, RUSSELL met Mrs. Maggs in the corridor as usual. "The wanderer returns!" she said. "Did you find treasure or trouble?"

"A bit of both," he replied. "I deterred a delinquent and made some discoveries. Time will tell which was the more important! I've got a lot of serious thinking to do in the next few weeks."

"They say one man's trash is another man's treasure. But you should think of finding your treasure in your relationships, not in your belongings."

As he went on his way, Russell thought, *She's quite the common man's philosopher today. However, I must also make sure they don't turn my fossil treasures into trash.*

Resuming work on his research project, he found that Zemki and Norman had made substantial progress. Having ordered two of the potential co-factors from suppliers, they'd also located preparative methods and ordered the precursors for two more. They considered the fifth one the most promising, but were still trying to find a source or synthesis for it. That was an exceedingly rare peptidyl steroid known as activinocrine, whose structure had only recently been determined. It looked as if a long and extremely difficult synthesis would be needed to obtain it. The team prepared for the purification of the four available co-factors as well as getting ready the biochemical tests for their interaction with the *longiferase* variants.

Russell started a search for a source of the sixth potential co-factor he had reserved for his own. In the evenings, however, when it was quiet in the lab, he studied his coleoid fossils, selecting one of them with soft tissue traces. Taking elaborate precautions to avoid any contamination, he carefully freed it of remaining clay matrix, cleaned it with distilled water and solvents, and removed a small portion for analysis. He extracted any undegraded proteins with a classic TCA/acetone procedure and rehydrated the extract with phosphate buffer solution. Then he used a mass spectrometric method to identify any intact proteins. The technique gave unequivocal evidence that delicate proteins including collagen, hemoglobin, elastin, laminin, and histones were all present. Based on his own experience of the difficulties of preserving proteins, even in ideal lab conditions, Russell felt convinced that such materials could never have survived millions of years in Wiltshire clay. The fossils must be much younger.

Meeting Ambi on the next Wednesday, he told her he had found the soft tissues in his crustacean fossils were real, and that he'd proved that they still contained actual undegraded proteins. Delighted, Ambi commented that it confirmed what she had been reading in creationist articles. "These fossils are supposed to be about 160 million years old, but this evidence says otherwise. It would be nice to have an independent way of checking how old they really are," she said.

"Yes. The soft tissues contain carbon, so radiocarbon dating should be possible. I suggested this to Prof. Olympia, but she said it would be a waste of time. I wonder what's needed for radiocarbon dating and how much it costs? I'll look into it. I'm going to include my protein analysis results in my final report on the field trip. It'll be interesting to see what she has to say about them."

Ambi told Russell she had applied for a summer job with the Heritage Forestry Institute. They had replied, offering her a place, provided she passed all her university exams.

The final event in Prof. Olympia's course was the week-long exhibition of the fossils collected on the field trip. It would take place in the paleontology lab and adjacent museum. The exhibits had been mostly prepared by technician Jan Parrott with help from the two postgrads who had accompanied the trip. They had removed the plaster from the fragile finds and cleaned away remaining rock matrix from all the fossils they deemed worthy of displaying. Identifying the taxon to which each specimen belonged, they prepared cards naming each and arranged them in glass display cases. A large map of the Wiltshire collection area showed the strata outcropping at the site and marked the places where each fossil had been found. Visitors could press a button to activate a video explaining how the creatures would have looked in real life. It offered a lively account of their supposed evolutionary relationships. The exhibition would last a week, but the main event was on the final Friday. Drinks and snacks would be available for the finale at 4:00 p.m. that day. The event was widely publicized, and it was hoped the public as well as students would come.

Russell dropped in for a brief visit on the Monday to see how his specimens looked. To his disappointment, he learned that none of his fossils with undecayed soft parts were on display. He asked Jan why she hadn't included them. "You mean those coleoid fossils?" she asked. "They were small and unimportant. We already have a museum display of fossil squids from the Jurassic that are larger and more impressive looking. Those specimens of yours didn't add anything to the evolutionary story. But see here, several of the larger crustacean fossils you collected, striking ones, are on prominent display. You've nothing to complain about. We've even given you and Lawrence credit on the display cards as the discoverers of the clay stratum where the best fossils were unearthed."

"What has become of my coleoid samples?"

"They're in a box in the storeroom."

"Could I claim them myself as souvenirs?"

"Sure. Come to the lab next week when the exhibition is over. I'll look for them, and you can take them away."

During the week, a trickle of students and friends visited the displays, but on the Friday around 4:00 a.m. a good crowd of about a hundred gathered, including the University Principal and Warden Sinclair.

Slab and Veronica were among them. By now he had returned from the hospital and was limping around with the aid of a crutch and his knee in a large brace. All gathered round Olympia as she gave a talk outlining the main events of the field trip and drawing attention to the star items in the collection. She said how wonderful it was, that the evolutionary history of animal life from hundreds of millions of years ago, could be traced in the fossils they had collected. Praising the students for their diligence in collecting, she particularly thanked the two postgrads who had given so much time and expertise in helping to make a success of the expedition. Then she invited everyone to pick up a drink and a snack and circulate.

The undergraduates had been asked to stand by their own exhibits and have a spiel ready for anyone interested. Russell was a bit surprised to see that Alastair Sheldrake-Smith had accompanied his wife. He came over to Russell's exhibit and listened as Russell talked about finding the clay stratum. "It contained a wealth of fossil fish, crustaceans and coleoids," he said. "I even found several small squid-like fossils so well preserved they had intact soft parts."

"Amazing," Alastair said. "Surely soft tissues can't survive for millions of years! Why aren't these fossils on display?"

"They were deemed to be too small and unimportant."

"I don't agree. I've always said I'm keeping an open mind about events from the far past. Your soft tissue evidence throws up more problems for Darwinism. It's disturbing how authoritarian science is becoming. Evidence that doesn't mesh with some supposed consensus is being ignored or explained away. There's also a worrying trend for all sorts of outlandish ideas to invoke 'science' in their defense. But tell me, are you making progress with your longevity research?"

Russell was surprised and pleased that he remembered. "Well, obviously I can't give you any details because the intellectual property rights belong to MoliMart. However, our initial idea of how to extend the terminal proteins of chromosomes didn't work out, but we're now putting co-factors into the mix and the signs are extremely promising."

"That sounds ground-breaking. I'll be interested to hear of how this project progresses. But I warned you about MoliMart before. That company's operating on shaky ground. I'd advise you to be looking over your shoulder at alternative avenues for your future."

Chapter 21. **Machinations at MoliMart**

RUSSELL HAD RESUMED HIS duties at Benedict Hall and picked up his regular fitness and other activities. At the lab, he worked with the research team to obtain and purify samples of four of the potential co-factors. When they carried out the microorganism-based assays to test their effectiveness, the results were promising. The tests showed significant increases in the longevities of the microorganisms with all four. However, the results were not sufficient to justify taking any of them further toward commercialization. The whole project depended, as far as the team could see, on the fifth potential co-factor. It had always seemed potentially the most promising. The team redoubled efforts to find either a source or a viable synthesis for the peptidyl steroid.

Russell visited the paleontology lab to ask Jan for his coleoid fossils, the ones they had deemed surplus to requirements. "I'm very sorry," Jan said. "Unfortunately, we inadvertently threw out those fossils with the other rubbish during the clean up after the exhibition. But don't be disheartened, I can give you something much better, a splendid ammonite fossil that we happen to have two of." Although he accepted the ammonite, he was disappointed to learn of the fate of his fossils. He remembered that Ambi had told him they wouldn't be valued and was pleased he had set aside two for himself.

Without anything being said, Ambi and Russell had resumed their meetings in the Bishop's Arms. "The report I wrote on the field trip has been marked and returned," he told her one Wednesday. "Where I had described analyzing the soft tissues and finding preserved proteins, Olympia wrote in the margin, 'Excellent work, but your conclusion that the fossils are much younger than Jurassic is wrong. There are special modes of preservation that operate in fossils and enable protein traces to remain long term.' Her faith in Deep Time is unshakable!"

"I got my report back, too, but Olympia had just written her usual comments of 'confused' and 'out of date,' and she gave me a low grade."

"I'm afraid she isn't a very objective scientist. Emotionally welded to her Darwinian theory, she doesn't take an impartial or detached view of things. Of course, that's one factor that helps her to be such a good communicator. But at the same time, it colors all her likes and dislikes, including her relationships. Her favorite people are those who share her beliefs. On the other hand, she despises those who don't. It seems you fall into the latter category." While they both agreed it was likely the case, they felt there was little they could do about it.

As the academic year end approached, Ambi worked steadily at all her courses. Lectures and tutorials occupied most of her day, but she usually found time for exercise to a video in her room before lunch. In the evenings she mostly worked through her notes and checked obscure points in textbooks or online. The possibility of the job with Heritage Forestry excited her, and she spent time learning as much as she could about trees. She had little time left for social events. Although she wasn't popular with the students on the paleontology course, guys she met in her other courses had shown a lot of interest in her and had asked her out on several dates. So far, she'd always politely turned them down, but she wasn't sure about the wisdom of it. She knew she needed more social life to keep herself from turning into a dull bluestocking. *Do my meetings with Russell amount to dates?* she wondered to herself. He didn't act like a guy on the make. Did he have any feelings for her? He was always friendly, listened attentively to what she said about religion, but apart from their unscheduled time together at the Benedict Ball, he hadn't shown any special interest in her as a person. Probably he saw her only as some sort of talking Bible dictionary. But she had to admit to herself that she felt strongly attracted to him. The chivalrous way he had come to her rescue from Slab had made a deep impression. Somehow she would like him to become more than just a friend.

At MoliMart the atmosphere in the lab began growing hostile again. Dr. Irma closely monitored everything Russell did and complained about the lack of progress. One day he was surprised when she called him into her own office. From her edgy manner he could see she was in a dangerous mood. "We have to conclude that any synthesis of the activinocrine that we need as the fifth potential co-factor would take us months or years and would only provide minute quantities." she began. "Zemki has been digging into the literature, and he's found a detailed article about it in Russian. The paper reports that it's found in significant quantities in the ovaries of post-puberty females. The amounts decline very steeply as the subjects mature, and particularly after they become sexually active. If we can find the right woman, we should be able to obtain sufficient quantities for our initial needs from her ovaries."

"Normally we would advertise for volunteers, but that's impractical in this case for a variety of reasons. MoliMart's financial situation is precarious. The company is supported by rich investors who are old. They are intensely interested in the longevity project and are continually pressing us for potential treatments. Commercialization of our longevity method as soon as possible is of crucial importance. It's essential for us to locate a virginal type of female and persuade her to allow us to harvest the activinocrine. She would be completely unharmed and unmarked in any way. No surgery would be involved. We have nano-robots able to navigate the smallest capillaries of the human body. There would be no evidence afterward that anything invasive had ever taken place."

"I'm sure that you're aware that virgins are rare species nowadays and locating them is not a simple matter. However, Zemki has identified someone called Ambrosine Amhurst as a possible guinea pig. He tells me you are friendly with her." By now, Russell was starting to feel extremely uncomfortable. Shifting uneasily in his seat, he felt a frown forming on his face.

"We want you to tell this girl, in a friendly way, of course, there is the prospect of a summer job with MoliMart. Convince her to come by for an interview and a questionnaire. We will persuade her to volunteer."

"How do you mean persuade?"

"At lunch she will ingest a harmless sedative. During the afternoon and evening, we'll carry out tests to make sure she is a suitable donor. The results should come in overnight. If they are positive, we'll harvest the activinocrine in the early morning. She'll wake up feeling fine and will be told we carried out essential cognitive tests under hypnosis. That she has just come out of the trance. She will never know anything different. Now we are relying on you to bring her here willingly and to reassure her afterwards if she needs it."

Russell had always known Vonvoigt was ruthless in pursuing her aims. But this horrified and outraged him. For a start, he was sure she wasn't telling him the whole truth. Far from being harmless, he was sure the procedures could lead to sterility. Barely suppressing his anger, he said, "What you're suggesting is monstrous! It's immoral, illegal, and probably criminal. It's a totally unacceptable deceit and a fraudulent invasion of the woman's persona!"

Her expression hardened. "It's foolish to take that moral tone. You should know there are no moral absolutes. The point is to succeed."

"There is no way I would be a party to such a plot against any woman and certainly not against my friend. It's a terrible plan that you need to abandon. By any standard it's morally and ethically wrong. Consult MoliMart's legal department. They'll give you the same advice." Then he stormed out of her office, slamming the door.

It was hard for him to settle down to any productive work as he thought over what she had proposed. On his way home he hardly noticed the burgeoning spring flowers, the crimson tulips, the budding rhododendrons, or the yellow gorse. Finally, he stopped for a few minutes under a white blossoming hawthorn tree. He began to calm down as he breathed in the spring-like almond scent, but that night his sleep was troubled. However, the next day Dr. Irma again called him into her office. Seeming to be in a conciliatory mood, she actually managed a cold smile. She even offered him a cup of coffee and a chocolate biscuit. "We've had a rethink about our plan to harvest the activinocrine," she told him. "We saw sense in what you said. It was too drastic and authoritarian. We've completely given up the idea of obtaining the material that way. Instead, we're going to adopt a multi-pronged approach. We'll continue with our efforts to synthesize the compound, and we'll advertise for volunteer donors. Perhaps, too, we can obtain the material from an organ donor."

"I'm relieved to hear that! Besides being highly unethical, it would have taken the company into unlawful territory."

"You can dismiss all such ideas from your mind," she said with great solemnity. "Continue with your research. Try to find ways to shorten the synthesis. You can trust us with the search to find a suitable volunteer. We'll be strictly legitimate."

As Russell left her office, he felt somewhat reassured, but he did wonder if she was protesting too much. Would the company bother to tell any potential volunteer the whole truth about the risks involved?

From that day forward, things began to go rapidly downhill for Russell at MoliMart. His experiments began to go mysteriously wrong. The water tube to his condenser became detached, flooded the area, and ruined his experiment, as well as damaging expensive reagents and infrastructure. On another occasion, the balloon of nitrogen he had attached to keep oxygen out of his apparatus, mysteriously developed a tear, again ruining the expensive ingredients. The shaker equipment oscillating his flasks accelerated dramatically, dislodging and breaking them. Russell was convinced someone was sabotaging his work, but Dr. Irma insisted it was his own carelessness. Each day she became angrier with him, waving her chart of the number of his mistakes and showing how they were increasing exponentially. She reminded him that his contract depended on satisfactory progress. After a couple weeks, she sent him an official written document warning that his work was unsatisfactory and must improve. Next, she brought him a printed copy of the latest pages of his e-lab book. Thrusting it at him, she pointed out numerous mistakes, badly drawn structures, and unfinished sentences.

"That's not the e-lab book I submitted," he told her. "Someone has deliberately doctored it."

"Nonsense! All our e-lab books are digitally connected to the central server. Our system is 100 percent secure. You must recognize that your work is badly deteriorating and take responsibility for it."

Russell suspected Dr. Irma herself, or one of her PAs, had doctored his e-lab book. Realizing that there was an organized plan afoot at MoliMart to terminate him, he started to photograph the pages of his e-lab book before submitting them each day.

In the lab, back at Excelsis, Sir George also had a word with him. "I'm hearing from Vonvoigt that your work is deteriorating badly," he said. "She sent me selected pages from your e-lab book, and I can see they're terrible! Surely you can do better than that! You're letting Excelsis down! If you have personal problems, you can call for help from the university health agencies. Excelsis has counselors who can help to sort you out. Go and see one of them right away."

"That isn't the e-lab book I submitted. Someone is doctoring it."

"Now you know, my boy, I can't believe that! MoliMart's IT systems are 100 percent secure. I've got full confidence in Dr. Irma. Don't develop a persecution complex. No one has any reason to damage you or your work. Go and see a counselor. If necessary, they'll find a specialist for you. Your work was first rate until recently. I'm sure you can easily get back on track."

Chapter 22. **Drugs and Dismissal**

A DAY LATER, WHILE he was working in the lab at Excelsis, Russell received a text message from Mrs. Maggs. "Someone has been messing in your room." Alarmed, he hurried to Benedict Hall and found Mrs. Maggs. "What makes you think my room's been entered?" he asked her.

"Come with me and I'll show you." Going into his room, she said, "I'm in here every day and know exactly how you leave it. The door to your suite is closed. You always leave it partly open. The papers on your desk have been disturbed as well."

While Russell couldn't see anything out of place, he trusted her, so he started to check around carefully. Everything seemed undisturbed. He examined under the carpet, under the bed, behind and above the curtains, and everywhere else he could think of. Finally, he decided to go through the clothes in his wardrobe. In the inner pocket of his overcoat, he found a plastic package of 25 small polythene sachets, each containing a small quantity of white powder.

"Well, I never!" Mrs. Maggs exclaimed. "Someone has planted drugs on you! It's a wicked world we are living in!"

"Have you any idea who might have been in my room?" Russell asked.

"I didn't see nobody coming or going from your room. But I seen that Zemki, what used to live here, sneaking around. I don't trust him! He might have done it."

"OK, thanks so much, Mrs. Maggs. You're a treasure! This could have got me into a great deal of trouble! I'm going to dispose of the stuff right away." With a pair of scissors, he cut the pocket that had contained the drugs from his coat. Taking it and the pack of sachets with him, he went straight to his Excelsis lab. On the way he heard the sound of a police siren approaching the Excelsis campus. Saving four for analysis, he incinerated the rest of the drugs along with the pocket. Then, wrapping the four sachets in aluminum foil, he put them into a jar labelled "ibuprofen" and placed it in the chemical storeroom. Then he carefully washed his hands first with dilute acid and then with detergent. A couple of hours later, two stony-faced police officers, accompanied by a German Shepherd dog, came to the lab and asked for him. Announcing that they had permission from the University Principal to search the premises, they walked the dog all around the lab and brought him up close to Russell. As with most research labs, a mix of chemical odors permeated it. The German Shepherd rushed around excitedly, investigating them, but didn't stop and point at anything specific.

When they prepared to leave, Russell asked, "What's all this about?"

"Just making routine enquiries," they replied. "Sorry to have bothered you."

The rest of the lab personnel had watched the proceedings with intense curiosity. After the police had gone, they crowded around Russell, asking what was going on.

"You know as much as I do," he said. "They claimed it was just routine work. Bringing that German Shepherd indicates they were looking for drugs. But why here? I guess they must have had an anonymous tip off from someone. Who would tip off the police to suspect me? Does anyone have any ideas?"

No one offered anything, but they dispersed wondering even more about Russell. First there had been the strange photo of him posing as Adam, next he'd been involved in some hush hush project with MoliMart, then rumors had circulated alleging he had beaten up an undergrad, and now this drugs business. What he was really involved in was a much-discussed topic.

Russell realized what a close call he'd had. He'd foiled a serious plot to blacken him, but was that the end of it? On his way back to Benedict Hall he bought Mrs. Maggs a large box of her favorite Dairy Milk chocolates. The next morning, he warmly thanked her for her vigilance and gave her the chocolates.

"Wow, my favorites! You're the bright spot in my life!"

She told him two police leading a large dog had arrived only minutes after he'd left. "They went to see Warden Victoria, then they all headed to your room. They had the dog sniff round for a long time. It seemed interested in your wardrobe, but they found nothing there and eventually left, looking disappointed. It was lucky you'd acted on my message pronto!"

"Dead right! I guess someone phoned them a tip. Do you think it could have been Zemki?"

"I do, but I couldn't swear to it in a court of law."

Russell analyzed a small sample of the white powder from one of the sachets he'd secreted. It turned out to be the same modified Rohypnol he'd encountered in Zemki's notebook, clearly pointing a finger of suspicion at Illovian. Several cases of date rape had taken place in Dunchester, and Russell suspected Zemki was selling the drug he'd manufactured. Had the drugs been found in his room he'd have been charged.

The sabotage and the doctoring of his e-lab book continued for a month at MoliMart. Then, when he arrived at the main entrance on Monday, he was handed a typed letter by the security officer. Opening it, he found it was a formal notice of immediate termination of his contract with MoliMart on grounds of incompetence. The letter said his grant would be continued to the end of the academic year in lieu of a longer notice. The security officer handed him a box containing his personal belongings and demanded the keys to his car and his ID card. Calmly collecting his things from the car, Russell added them to the box and turned the keys and his ID over to the officer.

The man carefully checked the car over for damage. "You'll hear from us if you've damaged it in any way. We don't want to see you here again. Get you own taxi home."

Russell phoned for an Uber and travelled back to his lab at Excelsis. Although hurt and indignant by such a callous dismissal, he was not too surprised. He'd known it was coming for some time. The intention to get rid of him had become plain since his refusal to cooperate in inveigling Ambi into their scheme. It would be a relief to get away from the hostility in the lab and the constant sabotaging of his experiments.

Arriving at Excelsis, he found an email from Sir George Faircross directing him to come to his office. Russell deposited his stuff, fixed himself a cup of tea, and tried to relax before complying. He had a fair idea Sir George was going to ditch him, too. After thinking things over, he decided that whatever happened he was not going to continue any sort of association with MoliMart. What had happened confirmed the warnings that Alastair Sheldrake-Smith had given him about the company's willingness to engage in unethical and illegal practices. Though he had photographic evidence that his e-lab book reports had been tampered with after submission, he decided not to show them to Faircross. By now he wanted out of the whole situation, even if it meant taking up a whole new career.

Arriving at Sir George's office, he found the man's secretary looking concerned and a bit sympathetic. She gestured for him to go in. Faircross pointed to a chair. "I understand MoliMart have terminated your contract. I'm really sorry this has happened. You made a very promising start in my group, and I expected great things from you. But you've not lived up to my hopes. Your work deteriorated badly in the past few months. What's come over you?"

"I've tried to tell you several times that my research was being sabotaged at MoliMart and my reports were being doctored."

"It's no good harping on about being persecuted. You should have taken my advice and consulted a counselor. In any case, the damage is done now. You can't continue with me on the *longiferase* project. As you know, you are due to write up your first-year Ph.D. report during the summer. This will be assessed, and you will be given the chance to defend it in a viva exam conducted by your independent internal advisors. There is no great hurry. Take your time finishing any loose ends and writing it up in the next month or so. I'm sorry, however, that I'll not be able to give you a positive end of year report, and you will not be able to continue in my group next year."

It was about what Russell had been expecting. However, to make clear his own position, he said firmly, "I'm sure damage to my work at MoliMart was deliberate sabotage. I don't suffer from any persecution complex, and I don't need mental health counselling. However, I accept that my association with MoliMart and the *longiferase* project is over. I'm thinking I'll look for a different Ph.D. supervisor here at Excelsis and start on a different research project. May I take it that you'll not stand in my way?"

Sir George looked a bit relieved. "That sounds a good way forward for you. I'll certainly not impede you in any way."

Excelsis University was in that state of anxious quiet that comes after exams have finished and before the results are published. Many students had gone home, others were waiting uneasily to hear their fate. Ambi sat alone at a table when Russell came down to breakfast the next morning. Joining her, he told how MoliMart had sacked him, and that Faircross was also banishing him from his group. Now that MoliMart had control of his *longiferase* project, they had decided he was unneeded. Somehow, they contrived to spoil his research and used that as an excuse to fire him.

Ambi was indignant. Reaching for his hand, she exclaimed, "That's so unfair! It was your brilliant idea! It's not right they steal it and heave you off with nothing! I'm sure you could take them to court and convict them of wrongful dismissal."

"I suppose I might. But I've decided I don't want anything more to do with MoliMart. I don't want a job with them. I can't bear Dr. Irma, and I dislike their whole management style. I think they're an unethical and exploitative company. Alastair Sheldrake-Smith warned me about them. Said they engaged in shady deals. My time there showed me he was dead right. Whatever happens, I'm not going back."

"But what about your Ph.D.? You said Sir George had sided with them and is going to drop you, too? Will you have to leave Excelsis and give up on a career in biochemistry?"

"Not necessarily. I think I have a good reputation in the biochemistry department. I got a first-class honors degree and have given talks at internal colloquia about the visualization software I developed. Several other groups have shown interest in it. I'm OK financially till about August, and while finishing off, I'm going to inquire around to see if another supervisor will accept me into their group."

"OK, that sounds hopeful. I wish there were some way I could help you."

"Thanks. Just knowing you're concerned and sympathize is a big help."

"I hope you'll keep coming to church. I always ask God for help in these situations. I can't help but think all your atheist and naturalist colleagues have let you down and exploited you! That ideology has so little to offer. I don't want to preach at you, but God stands for the opposite. He seeks the greatest good for every individual. At best, your research could only promise an extension to the present life. I think God will give you peace of mind in this life and unending life eventually. That's better than science could ever achieve." she ended with a smile.

"You're living up to your name! And you're very persuasive! But you're right. I'm disillusioned with the atheism I learned at home and at school. I'm trying to learn what Christianity is really about and if it hangs together rationally. Because I think experiencing it is an important part of this, I do plan to keep coming to your church. But what about you? This is a nail-biting time waiting for grades. How are you keeping occupied?"

"I'm helping Shuchun and Nthanda organize their stuff. They're getting ready to go home for the summer. It's amazing the things they've accumulated in just one year! Naturally, they are both hoping they get good grades and will be back in the autumn. They're trying to decide what to give away, what to sell, and what to put into paid storage. I'm also trying to prepare for my job with Heritage Forestry. That means spending time online, and in the library, learning all I can about trees, and about what goes on in the forestry industry. Of course, I'm also getting my stuff together to go home."

Impulsively, Russell clasped her hand in both of his as they were parting. For an instant she thought he was going to kiss her, but students clattered into the dining room and the moment passed. They just exchanged smiles in parting. Ambi tried to analyze her feelings. How would she have reacted if he really had kissed her? Her head told her she should have objected. Russell was not a Christian and might never be one. However, deep down she admitted she was disappointed it hadn't happened. She couldn't hide from herself that she felt strongly attracted to him in a way she had never felt for Daniel.

Chapter 23. **The Disappearance of Ambi**

THE NEXT DAY, RUSSELL encountered Mrs. Maggs as usual on his way to breakfast. "I hear they're going to sack you," she said. The cleaning staff always knew everything going on!

"Yes. MoliMart has consigned me to their scrap heap!"

"Not to worry, dear. They're a rubbish company. Everyone knows there's nasty goings on at that place of theirs. Some of they security guards are ex-cons. You're better off out of there. They can't take your talents away from you. This'll open the way to better things for you! Every cloud has a silver lining!"

"Thanks! That place and that woman were beating me down. I feel as if chains have fallen off me. The best is yet to come, and I'm ready for it!"

"That's the spirit, love."

Russell made his way to his workplace in the biochemistry department. The first thing he must do, he thought, was to assess what he could rescue from the research he'd already done. Then he must write up his first-year report. He was still getting to grips with this at lunchtime when a message popped up on his mobile phone. It was from Mrs. Maggs again. "I'm worried about Ambi. She's not back in her room. It's very unlike her. Can you come over?"

Rushing back to Benedict Hall, he met her at the door of Ambi's room. "She's practically always here at this time," Mrs. Maggs exclaimed worriedly. "Often, she goes out to get a sandwich or something for her snack lunch. Then she comes back to her room and before eating she does her fitness exercises in time with one of those fitness gurus on YouTube. She's very regular. And she's not gone away or gone home, because all her things are still here. It's very out of character. I hope she's not fallen afoul of some of they students. I know she had threats. What do you think we should do?"

A sense of foreboding began gathering in Russell's mind. Slab was still recovering from his knee injury and had exam results on his mind. Therefore, he doubted Slab, or his cronies had anything to do with Ambi's possible disappearance. The only other threat he could think of involved MoliMart. Had Dr. Irma been lying when she had assured him that they'd given up plans to "volunteer" the girl? Were her conciliatory words just a cloak to hide her actual intent? Had they got him out of the way to keep him from knowing where they obtained their activinocrine? As he thought back, he remembered the cold smile she had given him. Were her assurances just meant to deceive him? She was quite capable of that. The more he thought about it, the more alarmed he felt. Hadn't she said that success was all that mattered?

To Mrs. Maggs he said, "Ambi hasn't been gone long. We don't want to jump to conclusions. It's possible one of her friends waylaid her and asked her to share lunch with them. What time do you finish your work here at Benedict today?"

"I'll be off about 4:00."

"If she's not back by then, send me another text. Then tell Warden Sinclair. Maybe Ambi said something to her about this. The warden will decide what to do and if it's time to call in the police."

"OK. I've got a nasty feeling about this, and I'm not often wrong with me feelings!"

"Yes. I'm very uneasy, too. I've got an idea of where she might possibly be, and I'm going to investigate. I'll let you know if I discover anything."

Thinking furiously as he went to his room, he knew that he should really report to the police and leave it in their hands, but he also felt sure it would be a waste of time telling them his suspicions about MoliMart. They would be incredulous; and, worst of all, he had no evidence to back up his story. Even if he could persuade them to investigate, they'd act far too late to save her from possible harm. *I can't just leave her to face them alone*, he thought. *She's a very special person and has come to mean a lot to me.* He thought of all they had been through. Ambi was intelligent and courageous. They had become good friends. Definitely he felt there was chemistry between them. Should he try to rescue her himself? But the MoliMart premises were protected with high security. How could he get past the dogs and guards? Russell well knew that he was neither James Bond nor Superman.

I must at least try to rescue her, he decided at last. Having made up his mind, he determined to be as prepared as possible. On his computer he opened up the MoliMart website, surfed to the staff-only section, and logged on. They hadn't got around to removing him from the list of users yet. If they had seized Ambi, she would be in the old part of the complex, out of bounds for most staff, which everyone suspected was the site for conducting animal experiments. The thought made his blood run cold. It was a section of the website accessible only to the inner circle of higher echelon staff. When he clicked on it, it required a different password for access. He tried a bunch of common passwords—"qwerty123," "123456789," "11111111," "password123," "monkey," and "princess," but without success.

For several minutes he sat pensively in front of his computer, staring at the word "MoliMart" in their logo. Eventually, he recognized it was an anagram of "immortal." It came to him that the longevity project had really been of crucial importance to the company's program. They must have been working on it much longer than he'd known—practically from the firm's inception. In fact, they'd been gambling on eventual success. Then he tried "immortal" as the password, but it didn't work. Next, he added the most commonly used numbers, "123, 999, 321, 666," to the end of "immortal," but nothing responded. Just as he was about to give up, the idea of adding together the values corresponding to the letters in MoliMart, a $=1$, b$= 2$ and so on, occurred to him. Assigning the numbers to the letters gave him a total of 101. After typing in "immortal101," to his delight he was immediately admitted.

He located a labelled plan of the secret area, showing its layout in detail. Several years before, he'd helped with construction on that part of the complex, when his father had a contract to refurbish and extend it, so it was somewhat familiar to him. When he was able to distinguish an operating theater and its adjacent preparation room, Russell felt sure it was where Ambi would be confined. Searching further through the web pages, he came across the complete security plan. It showed where the security guards patrolled. Where the monitor room was situated. Where each surveillance camera was sited, where infrared sensor beams had been installed and their fields of view. The outside grounds had only four cameras, because two fierce dogs patrolled them at night. Quickly he downloaded and printed the schematic. Then he plotted a route to the preparation room, where he was sure Ambi would be, avoiding as much of the security as possible.

Going to the Benedict Hall first-aid room, he helped himself to face masks, vinyl gloves, and bandages. Pepper sprays were illegal, but Benedict Hall kept a supply of the next best thing, "Red Alert," for the use of individuals who felt threatened. He took six of them. Selecting a hooded jacket and putting all this stuff in a backpack, he set off for the lab. Outside it was a gray overcast day with clouds continually threatening rain. The air was damp with occasional drizzle and noisy from the soughing of the trees as the blustery winds shook them.

At the lab, Russell's mobile phone beeped, telling him that Ambi had not returned by 4:00. Mrs. Maggs was on her way to see the Warden. Thinking ahead, Russell decided he must have a female companion with him. If he found her, Ambi might be frightened and in need of personal attention. He couldn't involve Warden Sinclair on such a wild expedition, and he hardly knew Ambi's friend Sarah McBride, because she wasn't in the paleontology course. It would be unfair to involve either Shuchun or Nthanda because they were from abroad and on student visas. If anything went wrong, they would be in dire trouble. Finally, he phoned Melanie and told her the whole story, together with his suspicion Ambi was being held on the MoliMart premises. Horrified to hear what the company had been planning, she instantly agreed with his conclusion and said she was ready to help.

Chapter 24. **Peril at Pleasant Park**

RUSSELL PICKED UP THE modified Rohypnol sachets from the chemicals cupboard and headed to the local butcher where he bought two large chunks of beef. Then he took the bus home to Dunchester. Karl was working late that day, so Russell texted him to ask for a loan of his car to take Melanie out for the evening. His father readily agreed. Making half a dozen cuts in each chunk of meat, he sprinkled powder from the sachets into them. Melanie helped him pack a warm dressing gown, shoes, a power saw, chisel, hammer, a coil of rope, flashlights, and a towel in his backpack. They took an old mat and put it in the car. Finally, they drove out for a meal at a local restaurant.

There Russell found a quiet table, and while they ate, he showed her the security map of the secret part of the MoliMart complex and took her through the route he had plotted. He gave her three of the Red Alert sprays, explaining that the top had to be twisted first before aiming and pressing the button. "If we encounter one of the security guards," he told her, "I'll raise my hands, start talking, and move toward him. You ease yourself behind me and, out of his sight, get the spray ready, and take aim. When he's within about three meters, let fly."

They killed more time at the cinema, but it still seemed to drag terribly as they waited till it was fully dark. After midnight, when the streets were quiet, they drove slowly out to the MoliMart premises. Situated next to a large wood of pine trees, it was surrounded by a stone wall about seven feet high. Russell was glad for the blustery wind, because the sound from the trees drowned out any noises they might make.

He parked outside the wall at the place he'd selected as close to the best route to a side door. "Ambi is a firm believer in God and trusts Him to take care of her in every situation," he said. "I've never prayed before, but I think we will really need all the help we can get. I'm going to pray for God to open the way for us and to bring Ambi safe out of this."

"I'm right with you," his sister replied. "I'll be praying silently along with you."

Closing his eyes, and with hands clasped the way he had seen at Ambi's church, Russell prayed, "Dear Ambi's God, if You are there and can hear, we ask for Your protection and help. Please guide us safely through. Show us the best path to take and help us avoid pitfalls. May Ambi be unharmed and help us to get her safely home. Amen." Although they didn't expect any miraculous happenings, as they checked around to make sure the coast was clear, they did notice a mist was blowing in from the sea and shrouding the open grounds surrounding the MoliMart Complex. They waited a further twenty minutes or so to let it gather, then he declared, "Right! Let's go for it!"

Quietly they left the car and Russell shouldered his backpack. They put on their masks, vinyl gloves, and pulled up their hoods.

"What are you doing?" Melanie asked, as Russell went to the back of the car.

"I've muddied the number plates. Just for insurance, in case someone from MoliMart comes after us. They might try to accuse us of stealing something or doing malicious damage."

Russell took the mat they had brought and threw it over the top of the wall to cover the broken glass and barbed wire there. After scrambling up, he reached a hand down to help Melanie. Silently they looked all round, but could see no one. The mist hid them from the main building. As they approached the first camera marked on Russell's plan, they both ducked below its field of view.

In the distance they heard dogs start barking, so Russell got the meat chunks ready. Snarling, the brown and black Doberman Pinschers raced towards them. When they were about five meters away, Russell tossed one chunk in the air toward the first dog, waited a few seconds, and hurled the other chunk toward the second dog. Both dogs caught the meat in their mouths, but as they began chewing, they still growled every time Russell and Melanie made a move. The dogs wolfed the meat down, and as the drug began to take hold, their movements slowed until they subsided into a stupor. Russell hoped the dog handlers would take a long time before investigating when the animals didn't show up on their rounds.

"Phew!" Melanie whispered. "Lucky you had that drug, or we'd have been dogmeat." They gingerly edged past and toward a side entrance door.

Russell knew the PIN code to open the door from his time with MoliMart and was glad it hadn't been changed. They entered, carefully closing the door behind them. The corridor was dark and was crossed by an infrared beam that they avoided by crawling beneath where they knew it must be. Slowly, cautiously, and quietly, they followed Russell's route map, slipping beneath more infrared beams. Arriving at the restricted area, they encountered a strong metal door. The same PIN didn't work on this keypad, but when Russell keyed in "immortal101," the door opened for them. The place was quiet except for the hum of air conditioners and the distant clicking of medical equipment. No one was around. Moving past the reception area, they took the right corridor and could hear the sound of small animals shuffling restlessly in their cages behind a thin wall. They reached the treatment area around a couple more corners, but found it was behind a strong door with another keypad.

Melanie was becoming anxious as none of the passwords Russell tried would work. "Are we stuck?" she asked. "Will we have to give up?"

"I expected this, and that's why I brought the tools. This door is too strong. It would take all night to break through, but I remembered from when Karl and I worked here that we plastered over another unwanted door—a flimsy clapboard one. If we can find where it is, it should be fairly easy to get through." He edged along the wall to where he remembered it should be and began tapping the plaster. Soon he heard hollow sounds. Flipping his flashlight on and off, he thought he could see a faint shadow where the door would be. "This is going to make noise," he said. "We are well away from the security hub, but we'd better get our Red Alert sprays ready in case a guard comes."

Wrapping his cordless saw in the towel to deaden the noise, he attacked the wall. Rapidly plaster cascaded down, and the fiberboard of the door appeared. He worked till the outline of the door was visible, found where the lock was, and sawed round it. They pushed on the door, dislodging more plaster on the other side, and stepped through. Beyond it, a short corridor with two doors led to treatment rooms. From his plan, Russell expected Ambi to be in the second one.

When he opened the door, Melanie felt for the light switch and flipped it on. In the glare they saw a hospital type bed with a figure dressed in a hospital gown lying on it. Russell felt a wave of relief as they saw the unconscious form of Ambi with a drip attached to her arm. They had guessed right about where she was. She looked peaceful, innocent, and as beautiful as a renaissance princess. A surge of such anger flooded Russell's mind that he could hardly contain himself. Taking his smart phone, he took pictures from several angles, explaining to his sister that they were for protection in case of legal trouble from MoliMart. Melanie pulled the drip from Ambi's wrist. They struggled to dress her in the warm gown and shoes they had brought.

Just as they were finishing, they heard sounds of someone approaching in the corridor. Russell motioned for Melanie to step to one side of the door. She got her spray ready. The security guard entered the room and pointed a gun at Russell. Raising his hands, he yelled, "Put your gun down, we are here on official business!" Melanie let fly with her spray. Instantly a foul-smelling red gel covered the guard's face and body. The surprise made him stagger back and fall to his knees, dropping his gun as he tried to wipe the gel from his face and eyes. Quickly Russell grabbed his arms, twisted them behind him, and tied them tightly with the rope they had brought. Stuffing a gag into the man's mouth, he said, "If you keep on struggling and making noise, I'll have to brain you!" When he picked up the gun, he saw immediately it was only a replica of a Glock 22.

Ambi was still unconscious, so he tied her wrists together with bandages and hoisted her onto his back with her arms round his head to keep her in place. They secured the guard to the bed with more rope and exited as rapidly as they could. "They'll know there are intruders about now," Russell said. "We'll make for the car as quickly as possible, not bothering about the infrared alarms." Moving rapidly, they ducked out through the ruined door and darted through all the corridors to the side door of the complex.

The next stage would be the most dangerous. Both readied their next Red Alert sprays as they emerged into the mist. A dog was barking, and they could hear the sounds of a clumsy guard blundering around in the dark. With no cover between them and the wall, they had to cross the open ground as quickly as possible. Russell wondered if the dog was another one, or if one of the first pair had come to. When they were about halfway across, the guard's flashlight picked them out through the mist. Aiming his gun at them, he shouted for them to stop. Since they knew it could only be a replica, they kept moving. The guard ran, holding the dog on a lead, to cut them off from the wall.

"You take the guard and I'll take the dog," Russell told Melanie.

They slowed down as they approached the guard and made as if they were going to surrender. When they were a couple meters away, Russell gently laid Ambi down on the ground, but as he straightened up, he discharged his spray at the dog. Simultaneously Melanie aimed hers at the guard. The dog yelped and turned tail, galloping off in fright and upsetting the guard. He fell to the ground and was dragged away, yelling, and struggling to clear his vision.

"Quickly now, we'll only have minutes till they come after us again."

To their relief, the mat was still in place on the wall. The mist had prevented the guards from spotting it. Ambi was starting to move restlessly as they reached the wall. Russell gave Melanie a leg up, and she helped to hoist Ambi over. As Russell scrambled after them, he could hear dogs and more guards in pursuit. He yanked the mat down to prevent them using it. Reaching the car, he laid Ambi on the back seat, and asked Melanie to sit with her. As he started the car, he could hear the guards cursing and swearing as they encountered the glass and barbed wire. One of them threw his coat across the top of the wall, but by then Russell had the car in motion. He ignored their shouts, driving past as two were scrambling to reach the road.

In his rearview mirror he could see them speaking into their mobiles, presumably describing the car and its direction. He drove fast till they reached a more lighted area, then slowed down and circled around a bunch of the streets of Dunchester, doubling back twice to make sure they were not followed.

Ambi began muttering as she was regaining more of her senses. "Oh, my head," she repeated several times. "What's happening? Please stop the noise." She started trying to struggle up. Melanie took her hand reassuringly. "You're quite safe now," she said quietly. "Russell and I have rescued you from MoliMart."

"Then why are my hands tied, and where are my clothes?"

"Oh, sorry. We were in such a hurry to get away we forgot to untie you." Immediately she took the bandages off Ambi's wrists.

"I don't understand anything," Ambi said tiredly.

"You were drugged at MoliMart, and it will take a while for the effects to wear off. Don't worry about anything. Just try to relax and rest. Take some sips of this water and lie back. My brother and I are taking you home, and we'll be there soon." Seeming reassured, Ambi lay back, closing her eyes.

Russell felt as if he had run a marathon, but it was still only about 1:30 a.m. when they reached Ambi's home. The house was dark and quiet, but after ringing repeatedly, a wary Pastor Amhurst in his dressing gown opened the door. Russell was carrying Ambi, and he handed her into her father's arms.

"What's happened?" Amhurst asked. "Has she been in an accident?" With a puzzled frown he motioned for them to come in. Mrs. Amhurst and Rosie had appeared and were exclaiming as they helped lay Ambi on a couch in the drawing room.

"Best give Ambi a couple of ibuprofens with a glass of water and see if she can get some rest," Russell said, "Then we'll try to explain, but it's a long story." Mr. and Mrs. Amhurst half carried Ambi out of the room, leaving Rosie agog with curiosity.

"You've been having adventures, haven't you?" she asked enviously.

"Bold adventures easily turn into black nightmares!" Russell replied. "Poor Ambi was nearly the victim of a truly evil plot." Not believing in keeping children in the dark or sending them off to bed when there were unusual happenings, he added, "She was drugged, but we managed to rescue her. The effects should wear off in a few hours, and she should be OK."

"Can I come with you next time?"

He smiled to himself. "I'll see what can be done. It might be possible to work something out."

The Amhursts returned. "She's trying to sleep now. You must tell us what's been going on."

"Ambi was abducted this morning by someone from MoliMart. They planned to use her as a kind of unconscious organ donor," Russell explained. The Amhursts looked horrified as he continued, "Most fortunately, one of the Benedict Hall staff noticed she was missing and contacted me. I guessed MoliMart were behind her disappearance. Because we didn't have any evidence the police would listen to, Melanie and I decided to try to rescue her ourselves. We've just extracted her from the MoliMart Complex and brought her home. She's been drugged, but we're fairly certain she hasn't been otherwise harmed. By morning she should be over the worst of the drug, but you should definitely have her doctor give her a thorough health check first thing tomorrow." The Amhurst's had lots of questions, but Russell only said, "Melanie and I are terribly tired. We need sleep too. It'll be best if we all retire for the night and postpone full explanations till later."

"Yes, you both look all in," Mrs. Amhurst agreed. "We can meet again tomorrow. Can you make it back home OK?"

"Sure."

On the drive home, Russell said, "You were fantastic, Melanie! Wonder Woman and Florence Nightingale all in one! I could never have rescued her without your help. There were some very hairy moments, but you kept your cool throughout! You hit the bull's eye each time with your gel spray!"

"We're a wonderful pair! But I think we really did have help from on high. God must have subtly intervened on Ambi's behalf. Neither of us is a superhero, yet we got past those professional guards and dogs while burdened with her! Then that mist just thickened up when it was most needed."

"I think you're right. Several times Ambi's been targeted, but always she's been rescued! It can't be just coincidence."

Arriving home, Russell brushed the mud off the number plates to save on explanations. They crept in without waking their father. As soon as he reached his room, Russell sent a text message to Mrs. Maggs and another to Warden Sinclair. "Ambi's been found, and she's now safe at home with her family in Dunchester," it stated.

Chapter 25. **Aftermath**

THE NEXT EVENING, RUSSELL and Melanie went to call on the Amhursts. They found Ambi feeling considerably better. A complete physical check-up had given her an all-clear. She ran over to them and flung her arms around them both. "I'm too grateful for words. You've saved me again!" The Amhursts were eager to hear the full story, so Melanie gave them an account of the rescue, aided from time to time by Russell. Rosie's eyes widened with fright when Melanie described the approach of the fierce dogs. She asked to see a Red Alert spray can and turned it around curiously in her hand. Melanie gave her a graphic description of the sticky red gel and its horrible smell.

"Why would MoliMart pick on Ambi?" Pastor Amhurst asked curiously. Russell told them about the report in a Russian scientific paper that ovaries secreted a key substance MoliMart needed. He explained that the research team there had identified Ambi, from Zemki's descriptions, as a very promising source. Knowing the risks to her, they had decided to harvest it clandestinely. They had hoped to operate in a way that would be undetectable. "The next morning they would tell Ambi a cock and bull story about her being hypnotized. As you've seen, this wouldn't have worked. The drug was much more debilitating than they expected. And I'm sure the operation would have been even more harmful than they predicted, too."

"I think God must have given you the insight to guess exactly where she was and help to get through to her," Pastor Amhurst concluded. "It can't be a coincidence that you, the one to rescue her, just happened to have worked on the building and knew about the hidden door! I'm going to say a prayer of thanks." Everyone gathered round him and joined hands. "Eternal Father, we raise our voices in thanks and praise for the love and care You show to us humankind whom You created and redeemed. Today we especially thank You for Your watch care of our precious daughter. For rescuing her from a grievous snare. For saving her from the schemes of ruthless men. You are always our strength and our rock. We thank You for raising up these young people, for giving them the insight they needed, and for bringing them safely through the security mazes. We trust in Your promises and look forward to a time of peace and security in Your eternal kingdom. In Jesus name we pray. Amen."

The girls offered drinks and went to fetch them. "I guess the promises you mentioned about an eternal kingdom are in the Bible," Russell remarked. "I've been reading books vouching for its historical reliability. I believe that you as an amateur archaeologist would agree with that. But can the accounts in the Bible be reconciled with science? Are the teachings in the Bible rational and believable ?"

"Yes, archaeology has supported and illuminated the text of the Bible in hundreds of remarkable ways. I think science, correctly understood, supports the Bible, too. Furthermore, its teachings help to make sense of the confusing mixture of good and bad we encounter in the world. It's necessary to move outside the naturalist/atheist box that restricts reality to only material things. But that is hard to do, because this worldview pervades our society and has been taught us since birth. Breaking out requires courage and a determination to follow evidence rather than just modern consensus science. More and more scientists are coming to realize that Darwin's theory of evolution is a clunky old Victorian construct that's failed. As more and more is being discovered about the complexities of DNA, and the protein networks associated with it, so the inadequacy of mutations with unguided natural selection is coming to be appreciated."

As the girls reappeared with snacks, Amhurst concluded, "Now isn't the time to go into all this. We have a series of study seminars on Friday evenings at the Fidem Adventus Christi Church. They're dealing with the major teachings of the Bible. If you want to know more, you would be very welcome to join the small group who participate."

"I know quite a bit about DNA, and you're not wrong about the new levels of coding and complexity continually being discovered," Russell said. "The seminars sound intriguing. I'm seriously thinking of attending."

By Wednesday, Ambi was practically recovered as she joined Russell that evening at the Bishop's Arms. Her eyes sparkled and her face lit up as she approached him. "I don't know how to thank you! That's twice you've rescued me! You've been a mixture of Saint George and Oskar Schindler for me. I hope there's not going to be a third time!"

"I hope you aren't going to experience any unpleasant aftereffects."

"I did have a horrible dream. I was in bed and some monstrous, unseen danger was threatening me. Suddenly I was seized and bundled on to someone's back. We rushed through what seemed like an underground obstacle course. I tried to get away, but I couldn't move, and it felt as if my legs were in the grip of a vice. I tried to shout and scream for help, but only muffled sounds came out. We emerged into a gloomy courtyard, and as a huge baying wolf leapt for my throat. I woke with a terrible start."

"That's a dreadful nightmare! Yet it mirrors quite a lot of what actually happened to you! The vice on your legs was me holding you in place on my back! I guess you were coming around from the drug as we made our escape. I do hope that dream doesn't keep recurring! How did MoliMart get hold of you in the first place?"

"It was getting toward lunch time when I stepped out of Benedict Hall to buy a snack. When I reached the street, a car drew up beside me, and a guy I knew slightly got out. I think his name is Zemki. He claimed that you had had an accident at MoliMart and were calling for me, that things looked serious, and I should come quickly. Then he drove me to the MoliMart complex and escorted me to an office, where a creepy woman who said she was Dr. Vonvoigt, started firing questions at me. I kept asking where you were, but she told me to calm down and have a cup of tea while the medics saw to you. I drank the tea, and don't remember anything more till I started to come around while being carried on your back."

"I feel a little bit responsible," Russell sighed. "It was my project on longevity that started them searching for the activinocrine they hoped to obtain at your expense."

"Oh, no! You needn't feel that way! You would never knowingly involve yourself in such a dastardly scheme!"

"Yeah! There's no way I'd be part of anything like that. It's made me realize how materialists justify unscrupulous behavior if it enables them to succeed."

"Do you think there'll be any comeback or further attempts from MoliMart?"

"They haven't a leg to stand on. You could take them to court for abduction and false imprisonment. You can identify Zemki and Dr. Vonvoigt. I've got photos of you in their treatment room. The scandal would destroy the company if the story broke in the media. However, I'd advise that you take no further action. Court cases are always time consuming and the outcomes chancy. The evidence would focus a lot of unwanted publicity on you. And on me," he added as an afterthought. "See what your father thinks and go with his advice."

"How on earth did you guess where I was?"

"I don't really know," he said with a quizzical smile. "Perhaps there's a tenuous connection between us through hyperspace? Or maybe there's a quasi-material thread of dark energy linking the two of us?"

Ambi laughed. "Yeah! Must be so! I feel it myself sometimes." Preferring the tangible to hyperspace, they linked hands on the way back to Benedict Hall.

All the undergraduates were in a state of nervous excitement as the end of year exam results began to appear via the Excelsis online portal. Each student could only access their own results, but word spread rapidly among them.

Ambi and Russell met again at the Bishop's Arms to compare results. She told him she had top grades in all her subjects except paleontology. It devastated her to learn she had received a failing grade in that subject. Shuchun and Nthanda had both passed. So had Slab and Veronica. Russell told her he had passed OK but that it didn't make any difference to him, because he was just taking paleontology as a sideline. But he sympathized with her about her failing grade. "The trouble is," Ambi said. "I've now lost my summer job with the Heritage Forestry Institute. It was conditional on my passing everything."

"That's terrible. I think Olympia has treated you unfairly simply because of your religious views. You should appeal the failing grade. Excelsis has a procedure for this. You can ask for your exam paper to be checked and re-marked by an independent examiner."

"For sure, I'll do that, but it takes a long time. I'm afraid it will be too late for me to get that job. They'll already have given it to another applicant. I'm sure they had dozens."

"That's so unfair! It's completely unethical and unacceptable for university staff to let their ideologies bias them like that. Scientists should be objective and open-minded. We all have confirmation bias, but Prof. Olympia's so gripped by hers that she only accepts what agrees with her Darwinian preconceptions. Probably she's not conscious of it, but it makes her blind to contrary evidence and even actively hostile to it. The trouble is, it's extremely hard to prove anything! Do you have any alternatives in mind for a summer job?"

"I'll check around for cleaning work. There are usually openings there. I'm tempted to get a job singing with a band. The pay would be higher than for a cleaning job. I think King Inanga might find room for me with his band, or he might know of an opening. I'm not keen to go down that route though, because it means working late hours in clubs and bars, often with people who've had too much to drink. Sometimes it's difficult to fend off guys who won't take no for an answer."

"Yes. I can see the disadvantages." Ambi colored as he added, "A girl as attractive as you would need a permanent personal minder! Keep checking around, perhaps something better will turn up. I'll keep an eye open, too. Olympia has invited all the participants on the field trip for lunchtime celebratory drinks at her place. Are you going to go?"

"I think so. Even though she hasn't given me anything to celebrate, it'll be the last chance to see everyone again before we all disperse for the summer."

"OK. Let's hope she hasn't got any nasty surprises in store for us! I'll borrow a car from my father and pick you up and the same people as before."

Ambi was in a pensive mood as she headed down the cobbled street toward Benedict Hall. On the way she noticed Daniel coming in her direction. Should she avoid him, she wondered. Though she saw him regularly in church, she didn't regard him as her boyfriend. She even had an idea he now liked Sarah better than her. When he spotted her, he approached and took her hand. "I've come specially to talk to you," he said. "I was sorry to hear you had failed your exam. That's bad luck. But why don't you marry me and settle down? You're not suited to all that higher education brainwork. I think you should leave those ivory towers. You're always getting into trouble there. I know what's best for you and would look after you."

"Is this a proposal of marriage?"

"Yes. We could have a good life together in Dunchester. I have an excellent job and will soon be promoted. Then we could set up house together."

Marriage to Daniel would solve all her problems, she thought. No more hostile encounters with Slab and his odious cronies. No more struggling to defend her faith to the indifferent materialists she met at Excelsis. She'd have a home, security, and a good social position. Maybe she should take her father's advice and accept him. But then she thought how typical of Daniel his "proposal" was. *No declaration of love. No invitation to a meal in a romantic setting. No presents or even flowers. He just accosted me on a public street and presented himself as doing me a favor! Old fashioned and terribly controlling, he assumes he knows what's best for me when he has no idea of my personal aims or aspirations. In fact, he thinks I shouldn't have any, just leave all that to him. He'd micromanage every moment of my existence. Life would be unbearably dull and restrictive with him. And anyway, I don't love him or even like him very much.*

"I'm honored that you would ask me," she finally said. "Thank you for the kindly intention to help me out of my difficulties. But we have hugely different interests and aims in life. We would never get on together long term. Our likes and dislikes are quite different in so many ways. I enjoy the challenge of higher education and got top grades in most of my courses. And I'm eager to learn more and develop my talents and abilities to their limits. If we married, we would be forever quarrelling and come to dislike each other."

Daniel looked offended. "Surely you aren't going to turn me down! It's a great chance for you!"

"There are still three years of my course at Excelsis to run. Marriage is anyway out of the question for me till I've finished here. Besides, I thought you preferred Sarah to me. I've seen the two of you together quite a lot recently. You mostly take her with you on the Hope Food Share runs these days."

At least he had the grace to blush a little. "We're simply good friends and have been doing a lot of church work together. Don't let that fellow Russell turn your head. He's lost his job at MoliMart and his postgraduate position at Excelsis. I know he's helped you out of some scrapes, but he's an atheist and has a bad reputation for violence against students and even womanizing with the cleaning staff. He'll only lead you into more trouble."

Ambi tossed her head and looked disdainfully at him. "You're just repeating a lot of malicious gossip about him," she replied, brushing his hand off hers. "All I know is that he's rescued me from serious harm and always behaved as a perfect gentleman. Anyway, this has nothing to do with the present situation. We would definitely not suit each other. I don't love you and know I never could. I wish you every success in finding another bride." With that she walked away without a backward glance.

Chapter 26. **Opportunities and Omens**

SENSING HE WAS NOW unwelcome in Sir George Faircross' research space, Russell decided to write up his first-year report immediately while looking for a new biochemistry research group to join. From attending in-house colloquia, he already had a fair idea of who were the active and worthwhile supervisors. Prof. William Beaufort's webpages confirmed that he was publishing plenty of high quality research and was internationally leading in areas Russell was interested in. Beaufort agreed to see him the next morning. Russell cleared his desk space, assembled all his papers and possessions, and took everything back to his room in Benedict Hall.

Next morning, he took his laptop along for his meeting with Prof. William. He explained that he'd had a serious disagreement with MoliMart about ethics and that they had terminated his contract. Sir George Faircross had close ties with MoliMart. Their reports had poisoned his mind against him. They'd fundamentally disagreed about the direction of his project, so now Sir George wanted him out of his group. With his laptop, Russell demonstrated his visualization software for biomolecules and asked if Prof. William had a project he could join.

"I've heard MoliMart is willing to cross into questionable territory," Beaufort began. "I have a couple of projects related to the interaction of proteins with DNA that could suit you. However, it will depend on your maintenance grant. That was originally arranged by Sir George. If he's willing for it to be transferred, then I'll be pleased to have you join my group. I'll discuss it with him and let you know the outcome."

That afternoon, Prof. William summoned Russell back to his office. "I had a talk with Sir George. However, he gave you a very negative report. He said you had started well, but your work had deteriorated badly. He claimed you were unable to work as part of a team. That you had developed a persecution complex, refusing to seek counselling. He said your memory was unreliable and that he didn't think you were suited to postgraduate research. When I asked about your maintenance grant, he told me he had another candidate in mind for it, so it couldn't be transferred."

Disgust flooded Russell. Having assured him that he wouldn't impede him in any way, Sir George, behind his back, was now circulating falsehoods. Opening his laptop, he showed Beaufort a comparison of the pages of his MoliMart lab-book he had photographed with those Dr. Irma had circulated to Sir George. The differences were obvious. "I didn't seek counselling, because I don't have a persecution complex," he explained. "MoliMart decided to terminate me, because I openly disagreed with the ethics of their plans for organ harvesting. They doctored my reports and also arranged a series of fake accidents to my experiments. You've been present at the talks I've given in the biochemistry department. You've seen the draft I sent you of my written first-year report. I ask you not to be prejudiced by what Faircross said but to judge for yourself. Sir George is on the Executive Board of MoliMart and always supports their line."

Beaufort looked thoughtful. "I've heard rumors about the untrustworthiness of MoliMart, and I have always thought Sir George was a slippery individual. You gave excellent talks, your report is impressive, and I know the visualization software you developed is cutting edge. While I'm willing to take you on in my research group, there is still the problem of a maintenance grant. If one can be arranged, then you can join me. I will check around to see possibilities and email you about granting bodies you can apply to."

The day before Prof. Olympia's celebratory drinks, a savage storm thundered in from the east. Ominous clouds blanketed the sky and chilly winds swept through the streets. Trees roared declarations of war as they bent hither and yon in defiance of the blast. Forks of lightening flashed to earth, and the thunder rumbled angrily. Rubbish from overset bins and fallen tree branches littered the streets. The elderly clutched their hats and coats as they scurried to get inside. Columburgh changed from idyllic to inimical in short order.

The next morning, the day dawned fine, and summer returned. On his way to breakfast, Mrs. Maggs met Russell with, "It's fine today, but what goes up when the rain comes down?"

"Mist or steam, I'd say," he improvised.

"Good try, but the answer's umbrellas. So, what did one raindrop say to another?"

"Aim for a pond, not a puddle?"

"Two's company. Three's a cloud!"

Russell laughed, then said, "We'll all be gone soon. What will you be doing during the holiday period?"

"I'll be doing me bit here most of the time. Loads of visitors stay here for the graduation ceremonies. Then the place is nigh on a hotel for summer tourists till the autumn term starts."

"Will you be getting a holiday yourself?"

"Who knows, dear! I'm hoping Arthur might arrange something."

"Won't Mr. Maggs be with you?"

"Mr. Maggs took off more than ten years ago. He cleaned out our bank account, and I haven't heard aught of him since."

"I'm sorry! That's really tough. I guess Arthur is all you have now?"

"Yep. He's a good boy and looks out for me as best he can. You'll be off to Olympia's place later, I guess? Don't knock back too much wine and keep an eye out for Miss Ambi. She's been in quite enough scrapes already."

As Russell set off for Dunchester to pick up his father's car, he thought about how they owed a great deal to Elsie Maggs' vigilance. Once back at Benedict Hall, he dressed and met the others in the car park. He thought Ambi looked beautiful in a classic black dress with a short denim jacket and her hair in thick wrap-around braids. Nthanda had on her traditional African outfit with her hair piled on top in a large spherical bun. He and Lawrence looked at the two with undisguised admiration. "You two look stunning!" Russell said admiringly; and Lawrence echoed his approval. As they drove out to Olympia's mansion, a large car sounded a raucous horn and blasted past on a blind corner. They could see Slab driving with a party of laughing friends inside his SUV.

On the way up the Sheldrake-Smith driveway, they could see many fallen branches and a carpet of leaves from yesterday's storm. One of the oaks was a sad sight, lying prostrate with its torn-up roots sticking forlornly in the air. In the marble hallway, the girls went off to the cloakroom as Russell and Lawrence joined the crowd in the great hall. They helped themselves to snacks and a drink from the buffet and circulated among the throng. Ambi and Nthanda soon re-joined them. As usual, Slab was trying to make time with Olympia, but she seemed distant and preoccupied. Giving up, he and a group of cronies sauntered over to them. Ambi could see his knee was almost healed. Scowling at Russell, he snarled, "You creationist creeps had the devil's own luck last time we met. It'll be different next time! I'm going to beat the daylights out of you and hammer sense into your silly heads!"

Assuming an expression of skepticism, Russell replied, "So you think! But for me violence will always be an admission that one's ideas can't stand up to sensible scrutiny." Slab swung quickly sideways with a jutting elbow, trying to jog Ambi's arm and upset her drink over her dress. However, she instinctively shrank away from him, flashing him a look of distaste.

Just then Alastair Sheldrake-Smith began calling for attention by tapping his glass. Olympia asked them all to fill their glasses. Somehow, she seemed ill at ease. "Join me in congratulating all the successful students," she declared. "Then raise your glasses and drink to the one who made paleontology cool. Charles Darwin!"

Russell saw that neither Ambi nor Nthanda drank to the memory of Charles Darwin. He thought Olympia had noticed, too, because she came over to their group, saying snappishly to Ambi, "I'm surprised to see you here. You haven't much to celebrate. However, if you read your textbooks and study evolution more carefully, you should be able to pass at the re-sit in September."

"I'm here to celebrate the success of the field trip," Ambi replied pleasantly. "It was a wonderful experience I'll never forget! Finding those delicately preserved crustacean fossils was thrilling. Then, outdoor camping round a real fire is always delightful! I think we're all extremely grateful to you for organizing and arranging a life-changing experience for us."

Loud murmurs of agreement and several shouts of "hear, hear" erupted from those around them. Olympia looked gratified. "I hope you will all register for the advanced paleontology course next year."

As the group broke up, Alastair Sheldrake-Smith approached Russell. "I hear MoliMart terminated your contract, and that Faircross is also dumping you?"

"Yes, we openly disagreed over ethical practices, and they've unloaded me."

"A lot of people object to MoliMart's ethics. There's a storm gathering around that firm. It's whispered that a court case is being prepared against them by the Immaculata Carmelite Sisters. They allege that one of their sisters was abducted and experimented on by MoliMart, causing serious injuries."

Shuddering, Ambi closed her eyes and her lips moved silently.

"What are your plans now?" Alastair asked Russell. "Will this mean the end of your longevity project?"

"I'm trying to arrange a transfer of my postgraduate research to another supervisor. Prof. William Beaufort is willing to take me into his group, but a sticking point is the maintenance grant. MoliMart owns the intellectual property rights to the longevity work. It likely means the end of that for me, although I have another idea about how it might be continued."

"I might be able to help you. My company, Endgame Capital, owns a chunk of the pharmaceuticals firm AlternoPharm. The CEO is a friend of mine. I'll give him a buzz and let you know if they might be interested."

"That's exceedingly kind of you. I hope Olympia doesn't have some kind of problem. She doesn't seem her usual confident self today."

"The storm yesterday has badly upset her. It uprooted her favorite oak tree, the one she called her Tree of Life. It turned out to be quite rotten inside and collapsed in the high winds. She can't help thinking it's an omen. It's set her off brooding about her objectives in life."

Russell circulated the room, wishing all the undergraduates he knew an enjoyable summer. He came across a subdued looking Veronica and asked her what she would be doing during vacation. "I'll be going to my parents' home near London," she said. "I've got a job as a temporary assistant in an antiques business in London. I'm sorry for the way Slab behaved toward you and Ambi! I don't know what comes over him sometimes."

"I hope you don't mind me speaking plainly," Russell replied. "But why do you stick with him? You know he's doing you no good. Already you feel you have to go around apologizing for him. Look at him now playing up to Olympia."

"I'm aware. But who else is there for me? I've flirted with you from time to time, but you're only interested in Ambi."

"You're an interesting and attractive girl. There are plenty of fish in the sea who would jump at a look from you."

"None of them are swimming my way!"

"It's probably because you're always around Slab. Guys know his reputation and don't want to tangle with him."

"Maybe you're right. Anyway, I'm going home to London to enjoy a long break. I'll see you next semester."

Russell collected Ambi, Nthanda, and Lawrence. After thanking Olympia and Alastair, they set off back to Columburgh. Russell broached the subject of accommodation during the journey, "My stint as sub-warden in Benedict Hall is coming to an end. All of you have had a year in Benedict and will have to find other accommodations next year. Would you be interested in sharing a flat somewhere in Columburgh with me?" They were all in favor of his idea, so Russell said he would start checking rental agencies for suitable places, and they should do the same. Arriving back at Benedict Hall, he detained Ambi a moment.

"You heard what Alastair said MoliMart did to that Carmelite nun?"

"Yes! I said a prayer of thankfulness for my preservation!"

"I've never thanked Mrs. Maggs properly. If it hadn't been for her vigilance, we'd never have been in time. I'm going to invite her and her beloved nephew Arthur for a good meal at Dunchester Castle Restaurant. And I'm hoping you will come, too. Melanie will be with me."

"That's a great idea! I'd love to come. But isn't Arthur just a layabout who freeloads on Mrs. Maggs?"

"Well, the way she talks about him you'd think so. She seems to think he doesn't have a proper job. But it would make her happy to have him along, so I plan to include him. The semester's coming to an end. We have to leave Benedict Hall by the end of next week. I'll book a table for 6:30 p.m. on Tuesday next week if that's OK for you?"

"Perfect. I'll see you there. My dad will give me a lift."

Russell went to find Mrs. Maggs in the cleaners' room. The invitation delighted her. "Arthur will be so pleased! We'll make our own way to the restaurant and see you there."

Chapter 27. **Fake Research and Faith Seminar**

BACK IN HIS ROOM, Russell began checking through the biochemistry literature he intended to include in the bibliography of his report. He came across Sir George Faircross's name in the correspondence section of a week-old issue of the periodical *Nature Biochemistry Letters.* A letter from a top biochemistry group at Harvard referred to a paper by Faircross and Zemki Illovian. The Harvard group had been planning to use a new DNA polymerase enzyme as described in Sir George's paper. They'd followed the paper's procedure for isolating the enzyme. The Harvard group reported that, contrary to the paper's claims, they'd found it completely inactive. Furthermore, they'd shown the procedure actually produced a mixture of three enzymes, all of which were also inactive.

Russell's eyes widened in shock. These were seriously damaging allegations. Turning to the current issue of the same periodical, he found three more letters from three different international research groups. They also alleged discrepancies in the details of three more papers by Faircross and Illovian, asserting that images and graphs had been doctored and photoshopped. An editorial in the periodical hinted that there were doubts about the validity of other papers from the Faircross group. It mentioned that the most recent article from Sir George had been withdrawn, and that a small independent committee had been set up to investigate his research output. Russell remembered the phenomenal success of Zemki's research. Everything he did had turned up gold. It was beginning to appear it was due to widespread faking. Checking through his inbox, he found an email from Sir George, circulated to his whole group, past and present, asking if anyone knew Zemki's whereabouts.

When Russell sped down to Faircross's lab to talk to his five other research students, he found consternation reigning. They told him they hadn't seen Illovian for days. That they had heard from MoliMart that he hadn't been at work there all week. One student said that Zemki's flat in Columburgh was unoccupied. He'd completely disappeared. Several newspaper reporters had called asking to speak to Sir George, but he was always unavailable. Russell thought Zemki must have seen the first report, realized the net was closing, and taken off. *I wonder what will become of him?* he thought. *He's really a very clever, though unprincipled, experimentalist. I expect he will reappear, with a new name, at a research facility perhaps in the USA or one of the newer bio labs opening in the Far East.*

Russell knew he had to vacate his study/bedroom in Benedict Hall by the end of the following week. On Friday, he gathered two suitcases of non-essentials and carried them back to Dunchester. That evening he and Melanie went along to one of the study seminars at the Fidem Adventus Christi Church. The group of ten or twelve others meeting with Pastor Amhurst in a side room of the Fidem church welcomed him. The proceedings were friendly and informal. It turned out the study was to be about the idea of eternal life. In view of his research, the topic intrigued him.

Pastor Amhurst first passed out sheets with Scripture texts to back up his points. He began with a short prayer and then talked for about half an hour, illustrating his statements with a PowerPoint. People interrupted with questions and there was about half an hour for more questions at the end.

"Scripture teaches that when a person dies, they remain in what we would call an unconscious state until the time of resurrection," he concluded. "Human beings don't possess any immortal soul or entity that separates at death to receive either reward or punishment. That concept isn't found in Scripture. People don't *have* souls—they *become* one as they receive life from God. Of the hundreds of references to soul and spirit in the Bible, never once is either of them declared to be immortal, imperishable, or eternal. Indeed, only God has immortality. 'Human life is like a vapor that appears for a time and then vanishes away,'" he quoted. "Human life is transitory." Such a view of the human condition resonated well with Russell's scientific understanding.

"Do you mean then, that the souls of the wicked are not forever tortured in the fires of hell?" he asked.

"Absolutely. Those passages of Scripture that speak of hellfire always mean that the fire burns only until all is consumed."

It was a welcome revelation for Russell. The thought of a God who could torture those who displeased Him for eternity had been one of the factors that made Christianity extremely distasteful to him.

"Do you mean, then, that man is mortal and that there is no eternal life for human beings?"

"Seven out of every ten chapters in the New Testament make mention of the return of Jesus Christ. When that happens, the dead will be returned to life, and the righteous will be rewarded with life everlasting."

"How can we make sure we will be among those marked out for life eternal?"

"Scripture encourages people to seek immortality. It's a gift from God. Jesus Christ is the source of this gift." Pastor Amhurst quoted, "'For God so loved the world that he gave his one and only son, that whoever believes in him shall not perish but have eternal life.' Only faith in Christ is needed. Turning to Him, reliance on Christ, is all that is required."

Russell and Melanie made their way home talking animatedly. "I've always thought life was far too short for the myriad things I want to do and see," he said. "You know, when we die, politics or the state have nothing to offer us beyond that, nor does naturalist philosophy. The most science or medicine can offer is the hope, eventually, of some prolongation of life. That's all my research could ever achieve. Pastor Amhurst's brand of Christianity offers much more. It seems foolish to ignore it or denigrate it the way my atheist friends do. What is there to lose? I'm going to dig deeper and keep attending these seminars."

"I used to see no point in life at all," his sister replied. "But at the health spa, Dr. Regius showed us masses of convincing evidence that God exists, that Scripture is dependable, and that God cares about us individually. He helped me change my mind about the meaning and direction of my life. I'm hoping he will turn up at one of these seminars."

Chapter 28. **Mrs. Maggs Amazes**

NEXT MONDAY, RUSSELL WAS working in his room at Benedict Hall when an email from the human resources section of AlternoPharm popped into his inbox. It invited him for an interview the Wednesday of the following week at their headquarters in London's Dockland. He felt sure it was the result of Alastair Sheldrake-Smith's recommendation. But, cautious after his experience with MoliMart, he checked the website of AlternoPharm and found they claimed to be an independent company manufacturing and distributing medicines designed for the treatment of various degenerative diseases. The Financial Conduct Authority website gave them a clean bill of health, as did the government's Companies House website. Trustpilot and Google reviews had many positive recommendations and very few negative comments on their products and services. Finally, he surfed to the website of Endgame Capital, noted their contact details, and rang their head office, asking to speak to Alastair. His secretary told Russell he was currently in conference, but she would inform him about the call. At lunchtime Russell's mobile beeped, and Alastair came on the line.

"It was extremely good of you to speak to AlternoPharm on my behalf," Russell said. "They've invited me for an interview at their London headquarters. But what could they want from me? Can you tell me anything about the company and the purpose of their interview?"

"AlternoPharm is a sound and profitable business making top quality medicines mainly for diseases like arthritis, osteoporosis, diabetes, and cancer. They have their own longevity research program. Currently it's not making much progress. Their chief scientific officer was extremely interested in the little I could tell him about your work. I think they will want you to cooperate with them in some fashion in this area."

"The problem will be that MoliMart own the rights to the longevity research I initiated."

"I've heard a whisper that the American parent company of MoliMart is very dissatisfied with them. The court case I told you about is the last straw. They are on the verge of breaking up the firm and selling off the various divisions. AlternoPharm will buy up the rights to their longevity research and any assets with it."

"OK! That's very interesting indeed. Because I began to distrust MoliMart, I didn't share with them all my ideas about how to proceed with the longevity research. I'll go along to the interview and see what develops."

"I guessed you had much more in mind. Good luck at the interview."

Greatly encouraged, Russell continued polishing his first-year report and preparing for his departure from Benedict Hall. He started checking the websites of local rental agencies and estate agents looking for a suitable flat for next year. Then he contacted Excelsis' accommodations office to ask for their list of available rental properties. Finally, he went to see Warden Victoria and thanked her for all her help and support during the year. When he inquired if she had anything interesting planned for the summer, she told him that she was going on a cruise around the Greek islands. She would be giving lectures on the cruise ship and simultaneously having a culturally absorbing vacation herself. They wished each other enjoyable summer holidays and agreed to keep in touch.

On Tuesday morning Russell's mobile beeped and he saw Prof. William Beaufort's name. "You've probably heard of the suspicions gathering around Sir George's research group. It's a very troubling and potentially damaging situation for the University. Excelsis has placed him on indefinite leave, and they've set up an internal committee to investigate the whole mess. I'm on that committee, and you will probably be called to give evidence. One consequence is that the inactive maintenance grants that the University allocated Faircross have reverted to the central pool. Your maintenance grant was one of them. I'd say it's virtually certain it will be assigned to you again for research in my group."

"Thanks for putting me in the picture, Prof. That's really good news for me and a load off my mind. I feel really sorry for the rest of the postgraduate students in his group. What will become of them?"

"They'll be farmed out to other supervisors within the science faculty."

"OK, hopefully they can all find a reasonable fit and it won't be such a disaster for them. I should mention that I've been called for an interview next week by AlternoPharm. Apparently, they are very interested in the longevity research I initiated with Faircross and MoliMart."

"That sounds good! They're a dependable and profitable company. Several years ago they sponsored a student of mine. See what you can find out about their interests and intensions. Maybe an industrial sponsorship can be arranged."

That afternoon Russell gathered more of his stuff and set off for Dunchester. On the way home he bought a box of Mrs. Maggs' favorite chocolates and a bouquet of flowers for her.

His father willingly loaned his car, so Russell and Melanie were able to set off for Dunchester Castle Restaurant in good time. Melanie's health and appearance had greatly improved since she now avoided alcohol, was eating healthy foods, and had started regular fitness classes. Her complexion was clear with a hint of rose, and her hair was lustrous and stylish. He was proud of his sister again. "You look beautiful, Sis!" he declared.

"Thanks, Brother, you look rather elegant yourself!"

Russell knew several young men from the Fidem church were showing an interest in his sister. Arriving at the restaurant a few minutes before 6:30, they parked in the front and were shown to a table that commanded a view of the forecourt.

Soon they saw Ambi getting out of her father's car. Russell met her at the restaurant door. She was looking very happy. "I passed!" she said excitedly.

"Passed what?" he teased as he escorted her to the table.

"My paleontology exam, of course! As you know, I appealed the result. An independent assessor re-marked my paper, and they've given me a passing grade."

"That's wonderful," both Russell and Melanie chorused.

"Now I won't have to spend the summer studying and won't have to re-sit the exam in August."

"Brilliant! So, what will you be doing this summer?"

"That's still a problem. The result's too late for my job with the Heritage Forestry Institute. I rang them, but they told me the job had already gone to someone else."

As they were talking, Russell watched enviously as a luxurious black Bentley Continental S type car parked in the forecourt. They stared in amazement as the driver, a smartly dressed man wearing a pinstripe suit, white shirt, and colorful tie opened the rear door—and Mrs. Maggs got out!

The two entered the restaurant and, getting up, Russell escorted them to seats. Mrs. Maggs looked amazing in a full-length lacy purple dress with long-sleeves and matching half jacket. She wore a sparkling necklace and carried a small purse that matched her dress.

"This is my nephew, Arthur," she said proudly. "He kindly brought me in his car." Metaphorically, he hoped, Russell's eyes were popping out. "Arthur doesn't have a proper job," she added. "He's with some amateur sort of foundation."

Russell judged the nephew was in his early thirties. Of medium height, he had a pleasantly rugged face. Arthur's eyes twinkled as he added, "Yes, I'm with the Ancient Treasures Preservation Institute." That, Russell concluded, explained the ATPI monogram on his tie and on a small discreet badge he wore on his lapel.

A server brought menus, and they all selected three courses from the list. "What wine would you like to accompany your meal?" Russell asked. Mrs. Maggs ordered the simple white house wine, but all the rest selected soft drinks. "I'm not drinking, because I have to drive home. Is it the same for you?" Russell asked Arthur.

"No. I used to have a serious alcohol problem, but I got dried out at a health spa, and now I regularly attend Alcoholics Anonymous. The solution for me was to stay permanently on the wagon."

Melanie looked wonderingly at him and exclaimed, "The same thing happened to me! I was practically down and out till I reluctantly went to a place recommended by Ambi! Since then, I've hardly touched a drop." The two gazed interestedly at each other.

When their drinks arrived, Russell stood and asked them all to raise their glasses. "We owe a huge debt of gratitude to someone here," he declared. "It was her vigilance, her kind concern for the students she was cleaning for, that alerted me and Melanie, and saved Ambi from being butchered by MoliMart. Not only does she love a good joke, but she has a heart of gold, and she's our champion! So, raise your glasses and drink to her health." Suiting actions to the words, he clinked his glass with Melanie's as they all stood and repeated, "Mrs. Elsie Maggs!" When they gave her the chocolates and flowers, muted cheers came from other tables in the Restaurant.

Mrs. Maggs took it all in her stride. "Now, don't exaggerate," she said modestly. "I were only doing me job. Thank God, Miss Ambi came through safe and sound. There's rumors that horrible company's to be taken down. Good riddance, I says."

While they were waiting for the food to arrive, Russell asked Arthur, "Could you tell us a bit about the Ancient Treasures Preservation Institute? I haven't heard of it before."

"Well, there've been thousands of archaeological digs all over the country. Major ones like Stonehenge, Sutton Hoo, and Skara Brae are well-preserved and famous. But there's a host of others that, once the archaeologists have finished their work, get neglected, overgrown, and forgotten. It is a sad and serious loss to the nation. They're really national treasures. About ten years ago a group of archaeology enthusiasts in London were bemoaning this. They decided to do something tangible about it and set up the Ancient Treasures Preservation Institute to recover as many as possible. After establishing a small fund, they found some modest premises from which to operate. Over the ten years we've steadily grown, interest has blossomed, and we're now able to take on more and more projects. Our objectives are first, to identify certain important sites, restore and beautify them, and then open them to the public. Second, we're making a national digital archive/dBase of every single site we can identify. For those that are not important enough for restoration or can't be restored because they've been built over or destroyed, we copy all the maps, drawings, photos, and records that can be found, then enter them into the archive. We next prepare a 3D animated reconstruction model for each site to show what its buildings or structures originally looked like, and what its place in history was. So far we have several hundred now in the archive and expect to expand that eventually to two or three thousand. Perhaps, if there's interest abroad, we may go international."

"That's a huge ambitious undertaking," Ambi said, intrigued. "How on earth can you fund all that?"

"The UK government contributes a small grant. National and local archaeological societies give us yearly donations and access to their records. The public can join as regular or contributing members. Their annual subscriptions are our main source of income. This entitles them to access the archive and grants them entry to the sites we've restored. Contributing members help with site restoration. In addition, we have a number of extremely rich patrons who are enthusiasts about archaeology. They've donated funds for specific projects. The Duke of Eastmoreland is the chairman of the Board, and I'm the Chief Operations Officer."

"Awesome! What a marvelous job you have!" Ambi exclaimed. "You must have tabs on the entire history of the country as revealed by archaeological research."

"Yes, I'm incredibly lucky. Our headquarters are in London, but I travel up and down the country. In fact, there are sites we are interested in near Dunchester and Columburgh, so I always find time to visit my aunt here. But, enough of my doings, tell me what you are all planning for this summer."

As they ate, Melanie told him she was taking a course in business studies and working in the family construction firm in Dunchester.

Ambi explained that she was studying geoscience and had hoped for a summer job with the Heritage Forestry Institute but that it had fallen through. "I'm currently at loose ends. I might take a cleaning job, or I might go singing in clubs and pubs."

"She has a really superb singing voice," Russell interjected. Then something prompted him to add, "But you know her father is an amateur archaeologist, and she knows quite a bit about this herself."

"I might be able to help you," Arthur offered, looking at Ambi. "You're studying geoscience and have knowledge of archaeology?"

"Yes. I did well in almost all my geoscience courses, but my knowledge of archaeology is mainly about the biblical archaeology of sites in the Middle East."

"That might be OK. My institute is looking for two temporary assistants with basic knowledge of geography and archaeology to help with the archive. On our website there is an online application portal which also has applicant ability tests. If you can pass this, you would have a very good chance of a job with us."

"That sounds very intriguing." she said, an excited expression on her face. "What would the assistants be expected to do?"

"They're needed to search the records of local councils and local archaeological societies for potential sites. Do a preliminary assessment of the historical period, original ownership, condition of the site, current ownership of the land, and so on. The data will be passed along to our professionals to help in assessing the site's suitability. Assistants may also give input for the construction of the 3D animations."

"That sounds marvelous! I'll certainly have a go at your application tests."

Fresh fruit salad with lime sorbet arrived for Melanie and Ambi, chocolate fondant with pistachio ice cream for Mrs. Maggs, and vanilla crème brûlée for Russell and Arthur. As they were eating, Mrs. Maggs told them the dramatic story of the fire at Benedict Hall twelve years ago. While regulations strictly forbid smoking, a student had fallen asleep holding a lit cigarette. It fell and started a fire that spread rapidly. The cleaners had been at their homes, but Mrs. Maggs had seen the damage to two floors of one wing the next day. The local newspaper had hailed Warden Victoria Sinclair as a heroine. They had published a picture of her wearing a Greek national flag draped around herself. Smoke had overcome the student responsible for the blaze. Victoria had seized the flag from her wall, rushed from her room, and crawled into his, under the smoke, to rescue him. Thanks to her prompt actions no one was seriously hurt, but there was a lot of fire and water damage.

"She's a remarkable woman," Russell said. "She deserves a medal for her bravery. She's the one that keeps Benedict Hall going in more ways than one."

As they were finishing their meal, Russell declared, "We were depending on you for some humor this evening Mrs. Maggs."

Well dear," she replied, "did you hear about the first restaurant to open on the moon?"

"No," they all chorused.

"It had great food, but no atmosphere!" As everyone groaned, she continued, "Why should you never trust stairs? They're always up to something! Or maybe you heard what the tie said to the hat?"

"Tell us!"

"You go on ahead. I'll hang around! Do you know why the skeleton didn't go to the dance?" When they looked blank, she said, "Because he had no body to go with." Amid more groans, she asked, "What's worse than raining cats and dogs? Hailing taxis of course! Luckily, I don't have to hail a taxi, because Arthur will drive me home. They say, 'after supper walk a mile, after dinner rest a while,' and it's nearly time we all took that advice!"

Russell signaled for the bill and paid it. He had noted that an Excelsis undergraduate was one of the waiters, probably as a summer job, so he gave an extra generous tip as they left the restaurant. They watched as Arthur's Bentley glided away taking Mrs. Maggs home. As he drove Ambi home, Russell said laughingly, "I thought he was a layabout!"

"So did I!"

"Some layabout! Owning a car like that." Melanie added. "I wonder if he's married?"

"I've no idea," Russell answered. "We've evidently been misunderstanding most of what Mrs. Maggs has been saying about him."

"I like the sound of the assistant's job with his Institute," Ambi said longingly. "As soon as I get home, I'm going to find the Ancient Treasures Preservation portal for applicants and have a go at the test."

Chapter 29. **Ends and Beginnings**

THE NEXT MORNING, AFTER breakfast at Benedict Hall, Russell rounded up Ambi, Lawrence, and Nthanda to check out some possible flats for them to rent next year. Russell had prioritized a list of four. They walked to each in turn and inspected them inside and out. The first was well placed, but rather small and dirty. The second had four bedrooms and a kitchen/living room. It was within walking distance of the main university buildings and the rent was affordable. They would have preferred something larger, but the last two on his list, though bigger were more distant and more expensive. Finally, they all agreed that the second flat would be satisfactory. As they returned to Benedict Hall, Russell announced, "OK, I'll sign the contract and my father will act as guarantor."

Later, he and Ambi said their farewells to Lawrence and Nthanda who were both taking a shuttle to the airport that afternoon. They were flying home to America and Africa for the summer vacation.

Russell told Ambi that he would be leaving the Hall the next afternoon. "So will I," she said.

"Let's meet for lunch tomorrow at the Bishop's Arms," he suggested.

"Good idea: that will be nice!"

That afternoon, Russell spent further time working on his first-year report, then he went to see Prof. William Beaufort to enquire about his research group and the laboratory environment he would be working in for next academic year. Prof. William briefly ran through all the research projects his group were engaged with. He told Russell his project would be in the area of protein interaction with DNA. "However," he cautioned, "we won't make a final decision till we hear what AlternoPharm have to say to you. I have a contact at that company myself, and I'll get in touch with them. It may be possible to pick up on your longevity project." After he showed Russell where his workspace would be in the laboratory, he assigned him a desk in the write-up area.

In the morning of his final day at Benedict Hall, Russell packed up the last of his stuff. The place had been home to him for several eventful years, and he'd made good friends there. He felt a wave of nostalgia overtaking him as he went round bidding staff goodbye and taking a last look at the beautiful dining hall.

At lunchtime he set off for the Bishop's Arms and found Ambi already there. Buying sandwiches and soft drinks, they found a quiet table. Russell could see Ambi was bursting with news. "I opened up the application portal of the Ancient Treasures Preservation Institute yesterday evening," she announced. "I answered all the questions in their test and passed. This morning an email arrived from them offering me a summer job!"

"That's wonderful news!" he exclaimed. "I'm delighted for you. As Arthur described it, the job sounded exactly right for you. I'm glad you won't have to be doing late nights in clubs and pubs! I'd have felt I had to come along as a minder for you!"

"Oh, the clubs wouldn't have been that bad. The pay on this job is modest, but it will involve me in things I enjoy and give me transferable skills. I can't wait to get started. They want me to begin at their offices in London at the beginning of the week after next. I'll be going to London next week to find somewhere to live, and to meet their team at the headquarters in Brampton House off Piccadilly."

"So, you will be quitting your home and church and this part of the country very soon! How will Daniel feel about that?"

"Yes. I'll miss my family a lot, but I'll be able to find a Fidem Adventus Christi Church in the London area. As for Daniel, he transferred his attentions to Sarah. They're doing everything together now."

"I'll really miss you. I'll be working on my research here in Columburgh right through the summer. We've shared a lot of experiences together this year. Several were even hair-raising and harrowing. They've brought us together personally, but also, I think, on a mental plane. You've become a crucial and greatly admired part of my life. I hope you won't forget me once you're swept into the bright lights and sophisticated delights of London."

"Oh, I could never do that!"

"You know, I've always thought there was a cosmic connection between us," he said with a growing smile. "Now it may have manifested itself again! I've been called for an interview in London by the medical company AlternoPharm. They have a longevity research program and are interested in what I've been doing. It's likely they want to link up with Excelsis and sponsor me. If that comes off, I'll probably be spending time in London, too."

"That's amazing! It must be Providence at work."

"AlternoPharm's offices are in Docklands, a long way from Piccadilly, but if things pan out it should be possible for us to meet occasionally."

"That would be a lifesaver! I was a bit apprehensive of being alone and friendless in London. Not only is this great news for me, but it also makes the whole thing much more attractive. But I hope you will keep on taking Melanie to church here. And I really want you to stay in touch with my family. Rosie hasn't forgotten your promise to take her on an adventure, and she often asks after you."

"Well, it was only a half promise. But I do intend to keep attending your church and your father's Friday seminars. After what we've gone through during the past few months, I'm beginning to lose faith in the materialist worldview. I want to hear as much as possible about your Christian perspective."

"I'll be back in Columburgh next semester."

"Great! Stay as sweet and beautiful as you are now!"

As they rose to leave, Russell took hold of her hand and reached toward her with his other one. She took it, and they gazed into the depths of each other's eyes. Suddenly they were locked in each other's arms, kissing and embracing passionately, oblivious of the stares they were receiving.

After a while, he held her at arm's length. "I believe I have three routes to eternal bliss," he said. "The first involves my love for Miss Immortal Amhurst. The second concerns my research into longevity, and the third is through your father's brand of Christianity. Which do you think is the right one?"

"They don't have to be mutually exclusive," Ambi said shyly. "Test and follow the evidence wherever it leads."

"I definitely will! Some of the tests will be perfectly delightful!" he responded, kissing her again.

Printed in Great Britain
by Amazon

22620705R00096